The American Letters of a Japanese Parlor-Maid

The American Letters of a Japanese Parlor-Maid

Yone Noguchi

MINT EDITIONS

The American Letters of a Japanese Parlor-Maid was first published in 1905.

This edition published by Mint Editions 2021.

ISBN 9781513135915 | E-ISBN 9781513287508 Published

by Mint Editions®

 MINT
EDITIONS

minteditionbooks.com

Publishing Director: Jennifer Newens
Design & Production: Rachel Lopez Metzger
Project Manager: Micaela Clark
Typesetting: Westchester Publishing Services

Contents

Letter I

Pine Leaf San,—

I'm ready with my new adventure as a parlor-maid. Shame to be one, you say? Surely its helplessly pale singleness holds some romantic possibility.

No American servant is fit if she be not Irish, I am told, simply because the very first qualification is temper. I fancy I shall be quite at home in that respect. Haven't I enough of that?

(Did I scare you with such an abrupt beginning, without any sort of customary greeting? I have not wholly lost my memory of how to apologise with a bow.)

In the name of Lord Buddha, what will my "boss" look like?

I can fancy him heavenlily fat, looking even in the early morning as if he had just dined well. I shall advise him to assume the rôle of a Catholic priest. (Though I daresay no one is allowed to appear so outrageously innocent.)

He will return home with both hands full of paper bundles, giving me a chance to help him. His trousers should be a bit short, and his shoes should not be shined more shan twice a month. A large touch of carelessness in dressing should go to the make-up of a "Self-Made Man" of Amerikey.

Will he smile in his eternally patronizing style? So disgusting to be regarded always as a child! I'm growing awfully tired of American amiableness. If he could be unreasonable like Japan's Autumn weather!

Smart? Heaven forbid! Clever gentlemen are no longer to my taste.

Will he look reserved? Perhaps he doesn't know how to talk. Never mind! It will be worth while to deal with him surely. How interesting if he should prove himself a scoundrel by whispering me at first sight: "You are a peach!" Ho, ho! O ho, ho!

Leave such foolish thoughts, Morning Glory! Don't you know gentleman is only Mr. Nobody in Meriken household? His daily performance will consist of serenely filling a corner of the sitting room. Perhaps he will steal an occasional smoke behind the curtain. Funny, isn't it, law forbids smoking before "ladies."

WHAT A LUCKY GYURL YOU are, monopolizing all the delicious hours of Japan Spring!

Won't you pity your chum M. G.? Imagine a Japanese girl acknowledging the Spring without hearing the Nightingale song! It would be perfectly ghastly,—like no morning paper to Meriken gentleman.

Dear Nightingale!

How I wish to be in England just this minute, since Japan is away beyond any mortal reach! London gardens must be inhabited by my darling warblers. What if Keats deceived the world in his ode? Awful thought!

My uncle—"pocket dictionary", I call him, being awfully handy to appeal to in filling out the gaps in my knowledge—couldn't assure me whether English birdie would speak the same as our Japan's. If he or she (certainly not it) does ever sing the very "Ho, ho key, kio!"

Ho, ho key, kio, O Matsuba San!

Do you remember how we hung a lantern one night among the boughs of my garden plum tree, to show a nightingale one glorious blossom? What a fury I raised when no bird came to be thankful for our treat! I cried all night from my complete disappointment.

My sweet plum garden!

I dreamed about my beloved tree a few nights ago, and wrote a thirty-one-syllabled poem:

> *"Yume nareba,*
> *Sugata nakeredo,*
> *Kanbase wa,*
> *Omoino sodeni*
> *Nokori nurukana."*

(Thy sight did disappear, as it were only a dream, but here in my sleeves of fancy thy odour did remain.)

Is it too much trouble for you to tie the above "meagre" poem to one of my favorite branches—somewhere in the neighborhood of the sign—whose luxurious coil of blossoms sweeps the ground over the fence, like an American bride's satin skirt? The sign, you know, in my own handwriting: "One of your fingers shall be cut off for each branch that you steal. Beware, gentleman, your fingerless hand would be piteous as a care-worn old ladle!" My papa may have forgotten to put the sign this year. Poor papa! His forgetfulness is divine.

(Will you tell me, by the way, how the hair tonic is working on his head? May be it is only effective in the Ad., like the Chinese general in his report. How sad!)

How my plum tree would miss my slip of poem! It always accepted my annual offering with such a deliciously divine smile. If the blossoms should be gone before my poem shall "creep under your honorable knees"!

I left all my poetry with Japan. Dear Land of Inspiration, no more with me!

Adieu,
M. G.

P. S.—Mr. Consul recommended to me "the Autocrat of the Breakfast Table." He clings to an already tarnished idea that old book is always grand.

I right declared my disagreement with Dr. Holmes in baptizing his book. "Breakfast Table"? Fancy any gentleman feeling so comfortable at breakfast that he doesn't see where to stop till he has filled four hundred pages with his talk! Absurd! I'm positive no Meriken gent can afford more than half an hour for his breakfast. He is so hasty he sometimes forgets to pay a bill laid by his plate. "Summer Piazza Chair" would be a better title.

You will be horrified to learn that I skipped all the poetry. It is my opinion that there's nothing more stupid than to listen to another's poems. (I confess I take great interest in reading my own poems to another. Such selfishness!)

Second P. S.—I am thinking whether it is proper for a servant to take a trunk. My trunk is a magnificent affair, suggesting the owner to be an honorable counsellor particularly appointed by our august Emperor.

A Japanese servant carries on her back a few paper handkerchiefs and a night gown wrapped in a square piece of cloth, you know.

Third P. S.—My goddness!

I almost forgot to inquire, "How is your gentle self—I mean your Serene Highness?"

Letter II

My dear Matsuba:

How did I feel, do you imagine, when I went to see Madam for an engagement?

Do you know anything about a C. O. D. parcel? I felt exactly like one, trembling in tragic fear, having little confidence that I would be welcomed without any disapproval.

"I am an adventurous, sir," I said gayly, leaving Mr. Consul's.

Oya, oya! I had forgotten to take my Japanese cards.

645 Fifth Ave.

Wasn't number my aversion, ever since I suffered a nightmare at my school examination in mathematics?

How sad to see no silver-buskined romance in such an address!

How seriously I wished it were "Fifth Avenue Castle", not cheapening itself with any 645! If the castle stood half a mile from the thoroughfare! If a regiment of old pines began their parade from the gate, casting their heroic shadows like a design of Korin upon a screen! I would be tempted to plunge into the purple blessedness—ponderous as if with the odor from a dear idol's nostrils. Isn't it the place where your papa could recite his favorite song of Rosei awakening from a dream of worldly pomposity? How appropriately "There was only the sound of the pine-leaves" would sound!

I would like to know if there is anything more commonplace than an American door bell.

It's too unromantically prompt, isn't it?

I am glad, however, that no one but a telegraph boy has a right to strike very hard.

How dramatic it would be to call at the door, "I beseech my entering," as at a Japanese country doctor's!

The most interesting thing with my 645 is the "Stuart-Dodge." Isn't that hyphen great? I fancy that Madam would regard it as an insult, if you should ever forget to add "-". I hoped she were a Countess, but it was my afterthought that a Marchioness would be a deal better. Poor Countess is losing her favor in modern fiction, don't you see?

Mrs. Stuart-Dodge scrutinized my face through her lorgnette. She must be particular in her use of it, not confusing it with her "nose-spectacles", since she carries both. Is there any rule when to use them, I wonder?

What if her lorgnette were a microscope!

I felt easy presently, as the texture of my skin is my pride.

"My poor child, did you cut your finger?" suddenly she exclaimed, seeing a handkerchief rolled round one of my fingers.

Alas, no!

Wasn't I smart to hide my diamond ring under it? How I feared that its brilliancy might revolt, proving my unfitness for a servant's drooping-eyed humbleness! I might have locked it up in my trunk, if I had had a bit more determination. My handkerchief saved me from the dangerous verge.

"Just a little, Ma'am!" I said lightly, assuring her that it hardly deserved her attention. It would be fatal if she insisted on seeing my finger.

What a relief when she turned her subject to the everlasting servant question!

I readily imagined she might be an honorable member of a certain "Society for the Discussion of the Servant Question." She could gracefully fill the place of President, I thought, if she were not too busy inspecting whether the door of an ice-box were not open.

(I bet a doller if her present cook isn't careless about it.)

The first lesson in housekeeping, I am told, is to examine the door of the ice box.

How earnestly I urged her to give me a contract paper with a majestic stamp on it, like that of the Japanese government! Wouldn't it vindicate me from the slur of being a "dolly set in a glass case," if the paper were sent to my papa?

Madam laughed, not taking my idea seriously at all.

Isn't she lovely to pay me $5 extra a month for passing vegetables at dinner and washing dishes?

How she grieved over her second man's having left a week ago!

Am I not ready to do anything—even to carry a scrubbing broom down B'way—for money? Do you scorn your M. G. for her terribly quick Americanization? Why shouldn't I feel a little bundle of nerve?

I thought ever so hard how I should spend my extra earning.

My dear Matsuba, I was struck by a great idea.

I will walk down the chief Tokio street, may be beginning from "New Bridge," in my patent leather shoes and Meriken corsets, upon my return to my Japan. What a group of boys (dear street sparrows!) I could gather around me! There's no slightest doubt my narrow waist will spur their curiousity. I should not wonder if they might even ask whether my "honorable belly" were not rubber-made. What amazement they will undergo in learning that my shoes are not of glass! When I see their interest at its height, I will not lose a moment in throwing my thousand pennies over them,—my $5 extra being changed to pennies,—and crying out: "Boys, my worthy builders of New Japan, would you wast money in *sake?* No, boys! but buy land, buy land!"

It would be a lesson to them, certainly.

Isn't it romantic?

How shop-worn is the "returning-home speech" of a Harvard graduate! If the public knew that it was merely a translation of a Meriken editorial!

Mr. Consul and Uncle agreed that Anglo-Saxon's supremacy grew from their land-ownership.

(And another thing is their roast beef with plenty gravy on, of course.)

I can't help admitting once in a while that their learning is not altogether a failure! How sad!

How will my adventure turn?

The most dramatic part of it is my leaving Uncle behind.

Isn't it an event for a young girl to be quite alone in such a huge metropolis?

He wouldn't be an undesirable companion for a Japanese musume, but I ought to appear absolutely single as the heroine of a novel,—a Miss without a chaperon carrying a chain to tie her up.

The world is degenerating, I think, being full of wives.

What a magical word Miss is! It would be a sure prophecy that a theatre would fail if the bill were filled with Mrs. s.

I fancied that Uncle was playing a detective's part with me. How could I leave even my letter upon the table!

And the old Mr. Consul doesn't show himself so helpful, even with a pin when I need it.

"Pin? I never use it in my life," he declared one day.

How could a human being ever live without a pin, I wonder!

P. S.—Mrs. Stuart-Dodge confided to me that she has been suffering nervous prosration dreadfully.

It's a modern fashion to mention it, is it not?

Did I ever dream that the honorable wife of a Meriken millionaire could be so condescending as to speak freely with a Japanese girl ready to serve as maid?

Will not her "beautiful" daughter complain of her dyspepsia?

It would be mighty shame if I found her biting an inch-thick slice of bread with butter and sugar on it, behind the curtain.

What an excitement I had when I left Fifth Ave. with my success!

I didn't notice my shoe-string being loose, till I got to Mr. Consul's. Isn't it awful that I lost my gaiters on the road?

Letter III

I have made a discovery. I am a child no more.

I have found out my own soul at last. Isn't that remarkable for a girl who did not know it for twenty-five centuries?

Is this the 26th in our Japan era? Sweet old land of wooden clogs and honorably honorable bow!

It used to be my belief that a woman not equipped with the art of bowing showed a terrible gap in her moral foundation.

Poor Nippon musume!

Bowing is out of place in Amerikey, like a comedian's smile in the clear daylight.

I've given it up entirely, Matsuba San.

You will be surprised at the sight of my immense soul, when we meet again in 'Hama. The saddest thing about it, however, is that a girl with such a distinction will be a suitable candidate for the title of old maid. Isn't it a proud distinction for Japan that she never produced one old maid?

Mr. Consul begged me to take his carriage. How hard I tried to make it plain to him that such wasn't fit for any servant's part!

Uncle was ridiculous in insisting upon a retainer with his high hat to escort me to Fifth Avenue.

I could not leave any best hat for the world,—Meriken hat now taking the place of my tiny pocket mirror ("soul of woman" as it was called in Japan) next to my heart.

I carried my hat box in my hand.

Why should Madam oppose a girl's wearing what she inclines to?

And I did not forget my sewing box. Dear box enshrining all the carefulness of my girlish heart! I declare that Meriken woman does make me impatient in her serene unconcern over gentleman's lost buttons. Is there one whose morning work begins with her husband's coat, I wonder? Suppose I start a "Button-Sewing Crusade" in Amerikey?

My two gentlemen saw me off, sadly standing by the window.

I threw my kisses as I turned the corner.

(Miss Matsuba, is this not the moment for a curtain drop with a sudden volley of clapping from the pit? Dramatic climax of the third act!)

It was evening.

Purple twilight!

Could any hour be more appropriate for displacing a Tokio belle's kimono with an apron?

Mama was always so ready to blame me for stealing in by the side door of my home. Such a breach of propriety! Yet what a temptation!

I looked at Mrs. Stuart-Dodge's front door with eyes of envy now, thinking that no parlor maid might ring its bell.

Nell—the young lady's own maid, as I found out presently—ushered me in my room.

It was a disappointment not to find it the blackest cellar where all the servants slept packed together like sardins in a box. Wouldn't that have been the test for my strenuous endurance?

Very likely, I thought, Meriken millionaire may treat the girls as "ladies" whose barren lot incites sympathy.

Kind Amerikey!

How tall Nell girl was! Is she not cultivating the gentle art of shortening her height? She looked as if she would never get up to her original height. I am sure she thinks herself the real thing.

By the way, Matsuba San, "She's The Real Thing" is today's popular song in New York streets.

I looked around the room, thinking I might see a slip of paper on the wall—something like the "ten commandments for a servant."

An unpretentious pitcher upon the bureau by the looking glass—is there anything better to draw a woman's face than a looking-glass?—caught my whim.

I held it up, scanning a droll picture on one side.

Oya, the following lines were printed on its other face:

> "A trusty servant's portrait would you see,
> This emblematic figure well survey.
> The porker's snout—not nice in diet shows;
> The padlock shut—no secrets he'll disclose:
> Patient the ass—his master's wrath will bear:
> Swiftness in errand the stag's feet declare:
> Loaded his left hand—apt to labour saith;
> The best—his neatness; open hand—his faith;
> Girt with his sword his shield upon his arm,
> Himself and master he'll protect from harm."

What a foxy Mrs. Stuart-Dodge!

Wouldn't it be a capital idea, my Matsuba, to put a translation of the above under a new servant's pillow? You know the old saying that one dreams of that on which his head is laid. It might result admirably.

I promised to prove myself a competent maid.

I was summoned to Madam's audience in the library.

"O Cissy, look at Morning Glory's raven hair! Isn't it beautiful?" she turned to her daughter.

The young lady looked up at once, her hand impatiently fondling her pompadour.

Pompadour, my dear Matsuba!

Did you ever see one?

What an impossibility of hair-dressing for the Japanese mind! Its wild fluffiness rolls up tremendously from the forehead like an ocean wave. It looks a magician's bag from which you may draw out even a horse.

I have seen a number of extraordinary things about girls in this country, I do assure you.

"Did you dye your hair?" Madam inquired, looking in my face.

She was so prompt in examining it through the lorgnette, when I replied, "No, Ma'am!" "Is it possible!" she muttered. Did she acknowledge the colour was genuine?

What a deliverance not to see any austere family Bible on the table by the door! Its august presence used to give me such a wintry sensation, whenever I passed it at my 'Merican missionary friend's of Tokio. The touch of its pages was as with the freezing hand of an unknown divine being.

Warm touch of a crimson crime for me!

How often I said that no doctor of divinity—what a sardonic quietude the name evokes!—could be my companion!

Madam has none in her circle, pretty sure.

I saw no lazy rocking chair in the parlor, which will be placed in my charge from tomorrow.

When I glided away from Madam's presence, an old kitchen-maid whispered me that she was awfully particular about her pay.

"Pay?"

What a heavenly word that is!

Is she punctual?

How glad!

I was thrown in the desolation of my room.

The picture of a crying baby at my home "Alone in the World" appeared in my thought.

"Uncle! O Uncle!" I almost cried.

I woke up at midnight when the moon stole into the room, its whole light falling on the picture of St. Agnes maid of Keats poem which hung on the wall.

Lovely Madeline!

I left my bed to kneel to the Lord.

Do you laugh, calling me silly, if I tell you that I pressed to my bosom a horse shoe that I took from the wall above my bed, praying for my luck?

P. S.—The young lady is called Miss Cissy in informal endearment. She will evolve into Miss Cecilia by and by, when she appears to her dinner in a ceremonious low-neck.

Is it not your honorable self that underwent evolution from delicious Ma Chan to the present Matsuba?

What a free gayety Cissy (I beg her pardon) displays in her laughter!

What is it but God's mercy if we girls never die from laughter?

Her laughter is decidedly New York's—Fifth Avenue's in particular, perhaps—being luxurious, unsentimental.

Poor Japanese laughter—what sweet coyness it may be—is not fitting for anywhere but a bamboo tea-house.

Shiyoganaiwa!

22nd.

Letter IV

Am I not a born adventuress? Do you remember how once many a year ago you and I fled from our "small school" for a trip to the Marriage God Shrine? My preference was for a husband with a singularly great moustache. What indignation you showed when I revealed my wish to twist Mr. Husband's moustache while he slept! How we "crushed our soul" at the sudden sight of our teacher! Were we not quick to hide ourselves in an empty big rice-bag of straw? How I cried from the pain of having a bit of bran in eye!

O Romance!

Miss Pine-Leaf,—I got up this morning enraptured with the novel emotion of a successful rebel.

The rules for a servant girl should begin with one on being ready to a 7.30 breakfast.

(How modern for the kitchen-maid to whistle up a tube into each girl's room when it is ready!)

What an interest I took in my fifteen minutes delay before coming to the table! How often has my uncle declared it a crime when half an hour slipped by before my appearance!

I felt relieved, however, at not seeing one with a stick behind me to flog me if my meal were not finished on time.

None of the girls—eight altogether—knew indeed when to leave the table. I imagined they could go comfortably back into sleep.

They have such a heavenly satisfaction in face,—like a "ten-word actress."

What a pity for Meriken young ladies! They ought to cultivate a scratch of discontented expression above all things, since it is modern chic. Satisfaction is degenerating to stupidity. It is regarded as an unmistakable indication of genius if you complain of your insomnia.

How turbulently Nell laughed at the table! Her laughter was like a bursting bamboo.

Isn't it one advantage of being a servant girl that no one condemns it as an indecency if one does laugh even before breakfast?

When I came down to breakfast, all the girls were wild with enthusiasm in debating the subject: "Is Woman Higher than Man?"

Mary—isn't it funny 'Merican cook is always one Mary?—tried elaborately to impress us with her reasoning, holding herself as far above everybody else from the single reason of her industry in church-going. Look at a rosary and cross upon her breast! I am told that she would have been keeping her grace before each meal if the girls didn't "pour the muddy water over her." It is still Nell's suspicion (so she said) that she mutters it in the pantry. I wouldn't mind joining with you, poor Mary!

Observe the educated Ann!

She most divinely grieved at the corner of the table that the girls' ignorance of English grammar was perfectly outrageous.

She was an esteemed Miss B—(Ara, ara, her family name turned to a forgotten myth, only "B" remaining as a memory) while she was Miss Cissy's governess. The English alphabet hardly seemed competent to serve for her name, even with the addition of a few accents. Was she a Russian? Every Russian has an impossible name. With what an air of injury she explained that she was a pure New England girl. "Can't you distinguish it from my right management of 'shall and will'?" she used to say, as I am told. She was so sentimental in attributing her poetical imagination to her French great-grandpapa. When she left the post of governess to be a sewing girl—as she still is today—she shed bitter tears in throwing over her scandalously long name for a simple Ann. "That's better. Your name was too extraordinary for daily use, don't you know?" Madam must have said laughingly. And it vanished by and by. I am sure that her dignity was crippled considerably at the beginning. She tried hard to establish a distinction between her highly educated self and the others, exclaiming, "I'm unlike you, can't you see?" She looked fully pleased with the situation when the girls finally admitted her worthiness by dubbing her "the Educated Ann." She never finishes her speech without "I know, of course!" Is she trying to live up to her reputation? You can't blame her if she carries a victorious air as of the only one capable of solving problem, can you?

Dear other girls!

Weren't they born without family names? They must have left them at home, if they had any. They look eternally comfortably without them, like one in a light Summer shirt-waist who has forgotten about a heavy coat beyond memory.

Dear Matsuba, I'm one of them.

Wasn't I dying for a different page of my life, Pine Leaf San?

I greeted myself with perfection in my working order. Today! What an epoch for my family record!

Dear feather-duster!

Mrs. Stuart-Dodge did not engage me for my midnight eyes—for a curio to stare at—but certainly for my performance as a parlor-maid.

What would be the parlor-maid's office under the sun?

"Don't I know a thing or two from my living ten years with the family?" Marianna, the kitchen-maid, exclaimed.

Old Marianna of No. 9 shoes!

She has nothing to do whatever with the lady who was aweary and aweary in Tennyson's poem.

"'Tis too bad that you never learned French, isn't it? You could win Madam's favor without a bit of trouble, if you knew any. Even Canadian French, I should say, would do some service for you. Madam—you must not address her as Mrs. Stuart-Dodge, Morning Glory, it does displease her surely,—always says that French is the only language for her special idea. I am told that she is used to being mistaken for a French woman. Theresa, her maid as you know, would have been fired out many a month ago if she were not French. She has an awful temper. A French manicure girl (whom we call Duchess on account of her theatrical accent) comes every Monday morning for a treatment. She cleans Madam's finger-nails with the lemon juice. Don't I know a thing or two?

"What a nice lady she is you shall see by and by. Her Christmas gift for us servants is something wonderful. You must not mind that she goes round the drawing room every morning moving the chairs five inches to the left or one foot to the right. Madam has her own way. Why can't we let her have it? And occasionally she lets her finger run over the wood work of the wall. 'See, Morning Glory!' she may say, showing her dusty finger-tip if there is any dust. Oh, no, dear girl! don't you be so touchy with such a trifling matter! 'Tis the privilege of rich people to act as they choose, you know. Don't mimic her for the world, however funny she may be! Be sure, now, Morning Glory! It was last year that she hired May for charity's sake, after listening to her story about her lamentable husband. Poor May! She hardly thought that Madam was standing behind, when she imitated her, crying: 'There's one more fly, May!' It is superfluous to say that May was discharged. How Madam hate flies! One fly, she says, is just enough to make her dissy. She is very particular about the dust under a table. You must clean the drawer for dustpan and brush twice a week, to have it all ready for her sudden inspection. That's the place where Madam will judge of your availableness as a maid, Morning Glory. And you should empty your carpet sweeper every morning. Don't bang it against the table, if you please! A flower vase may roll down, don't you see? Everything in the house is tremendous money itself. Don't I know a thing or two from living ten years with the family?"

P. S.—Nell confided to me that all the girls have gone crazy with my beauty.

Isn't it sweet?

Lucinda, Swedish girl, keeps saying since morning: "Ack, ja! Vacker fliaka!"

(That's "My! What a lovely girl!" in Swedish, Nell said, Matsuba San.)

Dear chamber-maid!

What an incurable hunger for praise I am suffering!

Didn't I use to squander my pennies among the boys when they said "Beppinda, Morning Glory San?"

How I wish to hear it in Latin!

Who can speak Greek?

2nd P. S.—There's no dispute about my being one century behind. I came near ringing a fire alarm for the messenger. Thank God! Miss Cissy rescued me.

I sent a telegram to Uncle informing him of my safety.

Letter V

Honorable Matsuba Sama:

What a beginning!

Iya, my girl, you can't stand any such starched formalism, can you?

If you could ever see your M. G. in a white cap,—and with a red apron on,—in the morning!

(I ordered a silk apron yesterday.)

Such a saucy cap!

I am a bit shaken in my sudden fear lest it may be an inexcusable imitation of the crown of our empress.

What a delightful moment before the mirror!

Such a smile! Such greeting!

I should say that modern carelessness laid its hand even on a servant girl. My comrades leave their caps at the back stairway,—some girls hang it on the receiver of the stable telephone,—when their work is over at evening. Two girls quarrelled over the possession of one cap.

Matsuba San, I have decided to hide mine in the pocket of Mr. Stuart-Dodge's overcoat.

His harmless laughter makes me feel that I may do anything that I chose.

He wouldn't mind my putting a few things in, doubtless, since he deposits a heap of papers in his pockets. What are they, anyhow?

Are they his daughter's love-letters?

They may be bills to pay.

Oh, no! they must be a "Farewell-to-the-World" poem—why can't Mr. Stuart-Dodge be ready to die?—like the one under the helmet of an ancient Jap warrior. Dear warrior whose picture it was my joy to draw upon the margin of my old school book! I am told that he used to pay money for a poet to write the poem. What a pretence to leave the poem with his own signature! I laughed thinking over Mr. Stuart-Dodge's.

A gentleman good-natured like a boiled egg always keeps a trick, you know.

Dear Matsuba, you must now imagine me opening the front door, singing a naughty song.

What a gay Morning Glory!

How I wish to have a camera man passing by me!

Am I not charming?

"Dear friend! Aren't you a meadow lark?"

I exclaimed, seeing a bird dart out from a bush of the park. (The N. Y. Central Park dignifying the other side of this street.)

Such an audacious morning odor of the trees!

The bird, who undoubtedly had wandered out for sight-seeing of the Greater N. Y., didn't say a word. Poor fellow! He must have forgotten all his songs, like a poet who has left the country,—or like the honorable M. G.

Do you remember what sport we used to practise at our neighboring Mr. Foreigner's of Tokio by turning a mat to show the ever so cold "Exit"? What a cheap ready-made "welcome" on the other side!

I'm glad I see no mat at Mrs. Stuart-Dodge's. Gray-robed quietness greets you as you enter the vestibule. Delicious restlessness of the Japan house sounds to me now as a far-off stir in some unknown fairy-book. Here, grandeur, eternally changeless!

I bet you if you are not surprised at your sudden encounter with a woman's statue, with the "faith and bliss of Eden in her face," symbolising Spring throwing off the mantle of winter.

"And with a smile of gladness,
Greets the cuckoo song again."

What a poetry-smelling hall!

Won't you rest for a while reclining upon an ancient bench looking a relic as from a buried abbey?

You will shortly be captured by certain purple gossamers of fancy.

I wonder if there is any worse background than a Meriken wall paper for a Japanese girl? What fatality if it were painted with red roses and green leaves!

Pray, congratulate me on not being locked in a third-rate Merican boarding house!

What straight forwardness in the drapery coming down from the high ceiling!

The floor is flagged with minute artifice. John washes it with water, and with milk on Saturday, as I am told. What extravagance!

John is awfully funny, Matsuba!

Nell said that she had never caught him in his working moment. If he doesn't say "I am just going to work" there is no smallest doubt that it will be "I am just coming from work." He devotes a considerable time to his profound meditation as to whether the weather is on the whole favorable to his work.

He exhibits an extraordinary affection for his watch, bought in his "better days," but Mary the cook serenely snaps at it, calling it an "old-fashioned tea kettle." Whenever I see him, he is bringing out his honorable watch from his waistcoat, and opening its cover. He will glance over the movement a moment or two, and then he will listen to its tick-tack, even pushing it to his ear.

It wouldn't be any wonder if his watch were pointing always to 12:30, as that is the very moment for his quitting his work.

When the evening duskiness "hath in her sober livery all things clad," it will be the time for the parlor-maid (Morning Glory) to put the light to the Japanese stationary paper lamps in the hall.

By the way, Mr. Stuart-Dodge is a mighty enthusiast of Nippon art, as Madan says.

Dear classical shokudai!

The sight should carry my thought away back to the gracious wantonness of mediæval Japan, where Love and Romance strolled long one same road.

How I wish I could be lazy—certainly with my imaginary Miss Pine Leaf—under their lovely-eyed light!

Don't I know that even the homeliest can show herself a beauty in such a pose?

What a pity for M. G., whose evening as a maid is thrown in the whirlwind of American "Hurry up!"

Did you ever hear "hurry up" in your life?

Such an eternally dozing Japan!

What a new meaning in the word!

I accept it as the up-to-date tribute of a young land toward an older one.

I can swear to you that my aristocracy has never been hurt since my stepping on this Amerikey.

By and by, the hall clock will chronicle round half-past eight. What a sweet westminster chime!

(My first admiration at Mrs. Stuart-Dodge's was that no clock was out of order. "How is it possible!" you will exclaim when you learn that there are more than twenty. I have no knowledge of anything more sad than a broken clock. What a heart-rending sight!—like a wounded soldier. No one, I affirmed, could approach Meriken servant's endeavour in maintaining order. How sorry I was, however, at being so hasty in appraising it, when I was told that a professional watchmaker comes to attend to them every Saturday. Alas!)

Presently you shall hear the footsteps of Miss Cissy,—her new shoes sounding a "funeral march," as she expresses it laughingly—coming down the stairs with her puss.

Listen to her singing:

"Tell me, pretty maiden, are there any more at home like you?
There are a few, kind sir, but simple girls, and proper too."

Beloved Zara purring like a thrashing machine (borrowing the young lady's figure of speech)!

Certainly 'tis her time to be put in her bed in the cellar.

She gave me the very first welcome standing at the side entrance, didn't she?

Encouragement, also!

If the cat who can never settle herself comfortably without a glorifying hearth could ever feel at home in a modern 'Merican household with a radiator—fancy the cat purring round the snoring pipes!—why in the world cannot a Jap girl, I thought, manage to feel herself nicely situated?

I'm hugely pleased now, seeing a successful light on my new adventure.

There was one more pussy beside Zara.

"'Tis another story," Marianna said like a popular novelist.

What story, for heaven's sake!

P. S.—My little head is over-crowded with ideas that I will take up when I return to Tokio. One thing will be the translation of Meriken song. What fun if I could popularise it among the geisha girls of gallant Shinbashi!

Will you see whether the following be transferable to a shamisen?

2nd P. S.—The first thing we women like to know is where a closet is placed.

A house with the closets properly placed is like a clever woman who is trained where to stop her talk.

Miss Pine Leaf, I stole into Mr. Stuart-Dodge's closet by the front door tonight to examine his coat-buttons.

What a disappointment if they were all tight!

God was kind, giving me a chance to accomplish my "duty."

Do you accuse me of wickedness for thrusting my hand in one of his coat pockets?

Alas! I found only toothpicks. How sad!

I carried his worn-out shoe up to my bedroom, hiding it under my apron.

The way shoes are worn reveals temperament as clearly as a palm.

How about Mr. Stuart-Dodge?

Letter VI

Dear Pine Leaf:

Cissy—she would be glad to be called so, I bet you. Didn't we exchange our confidential wink?—will come down to her breakfast, crying:

"I am hungly as a wolf, papa."

The idea!

Did you ever? (Allow me to use one of her flashy expressions.)

Imagine a Nippon musume comparing herself with such a "four legs" with eyes murderous like fire! Isn't it awful?

How can any woman be hungry in the morning?

I dare say that no one in Japan except a carrot-armed washer woman is allowed to display her emptiness of stomach before noon.

Poor ever so hungly Miss Cecilia!

If her only joy were in eating a whole lot?

I never saw her leave the table without swallowing a lump of sugar and dropping her handkerchief.

One thing forbidden to a servant girl is that verily interesting dropping.

It wouldn't be worth while for you to try it, of course, with no butler to pick it up with "Handkerchief, Madam." It would even be ghastly like an actress exit with no clapping.

Mr. Heine—dear poet-friend of mine—once opened a box full of handkerchiefs which had been dropped by picknicking girls amid the grasses upon his Heights. O glorious Heights of sunset and breeze! "Day will be short—Heaven knows—when man takes to mending girl's carelessness," he snapped.

Did I tell you anything about Mr. Heine?

He is sadly labelled "grey-old." There's no question about that, but the funniest thing is that every poet turns at once from "young to "old." Is there no middle-aged poet, I wonder?

I laughed thinking whether those girls will ever leave their children in the wood when they grow to motherhood.

My goodness!

I wish Mr. Stuart-Dodge wouldn't look so happy at his breakfast table!

What disgust I used to betray at the early cry of a crow among the pines of my back yard!

"The old crow of Fifth Ave." is the title I playfully chose for Mr. Stuart-Dodge.

He scarcely loses a moment in volleying a song like "A Runaway Train's in the Desert" (according to John) when he gets up in the morning. The cook Mary complains that her bread-dough will turn sour from such a scandalous voice. Madam's training of her husband is so admirable, however, that he dares not express his rapture in singing anywhere but in his own bathroom. I'm sure he doesn't forget to even lock the door.

If you will peep in at the keyhole by and by, when his song has stopped, you will encounter the sight of him weighing himself to ascertain how much breakfast he shall eat. Doesn't one pound's loss mean two extra chops?

I am inclined to be displeased with the gentleman happy from early morning. Laughter and humor should not appear before afternoon tea, surely. Dear Japanese three o'clock when any servant as well as our Empress may savor the delight of green leaves raised in mountain air!

I am certain that Dr. Holmes had such a gentleman in his fancy when he penned his book.

I shouldn't wonder if the world would taste another delight in a book of the New Autocrat.

I will try to discover whether Mr. Stuart-Dodge is not hiding his venerable grey cap of Dr. somewhere.

Why doesn't he raise whiskers?—as necessary a signboard to an autocrat as a shaved eyebrow to a Japanese wife.

I don't mind a bit hearing his "That reminds me" or "Quite a number of years ago," although it does blow a breeze of agedness. A gentle touch of such a breeze cannot be other than pleasing.

How glad I am not to see him with his hands tied upon his back, coughing every ten minutes!

Such a show would pull me back into the fatal decrepitude of old Japan, doubtless.

Matsuba San, he doesn't wear any "dotard's cap" with the customary red ribbon on it.

Henry, the English bulter, is ever wondering how much the millionaire's family can eat.

You will not be surprised when you learn how the breakfast room looks. Every inch of the room would increase your appetite, like a summer piazza where no long stay is charged as a crime.

Look at those flowers!

The golden tulips ("Yellow Princess" is Madam's favorite, I am told) were abundantly diffused this morning. What a joyful blaze! Yesterday the carnations made a service. Madam would not object to a few stalks of lilies of the valley, bashful like a lass. Poor "American Beauty" rose! It flatly lost her favor from the singular reason of its perfection. "Is there any more commonplace flower than the American Beauty? I beg of you not to fight for its beauty. Alas, too perfect, almost losing its characteristic significance! It is sad it has no intelligence, no interior, my dear," she said. Isn't she one longing after an "ugly beauty," like an artist?

Pine Leaf, you are also a worshipper of beauty in imperfection, aren't you?

If you will leave the tulips upon the table and turn your eyes upward, your face is against the ocean—a painting by a certain Harrison.

Your imaginative ears shall hear the vast music of its eternal roll.

(Dear Golden Gate of California!)

What buoyancy uplifted me as I sat by the sea, feeling "what I can ne'er express, yet cannot all conceal!"

"Mama, can I have one more cup of coffee?" Miss Cissy will say demurely.

"No, dear! It spoils your skin. Didn't Doctor tell you so?" Madam will deny her request.

(Lucinda scoffs at the idiocy of her belief, even saying: "American doctor can't get money if he doesn't advise something,—no matter what it be. Ha, ha, ja!" She emphasized her words by citing the fairness of Swedish girls in spite of their much drinking of coffee. She didn't even mind carrying her "Sweden and Swedish" from her room as a reference. What a white face Lucinda girl has!)

There's nothing more ridiculous than Meriken woman's belief in doctors. And another piece of sentimentalism is her fancy for minister as an authority. Awfully funny, Matsuba!

Madam will summon her cook to give the day's bill of fare, when the breakfast is over.

And the rest of her forenoon will be taken up with the task of dividing the flowers among her own relations and the hospitals.

Isn't she lovely?

Alice, the laundress, almost cried in praising her! "She's the most varchous faymale in the wurrld."

Such Miss Cissy!

She whispered me entreating me to get a cup of coffee and hide it behind a Japanese stone idol standing in the dusky passage-way from the drawing room to a greenhouse.

Dear O Jizo Sama!

"Don't you feel lonely, being exiled from the land of lanterns and prayer? Yes, you do, my poor friend! Be honest unto me! How many people ever speak to you, I wonder, in your American days?" I lovingly tapped his back.

Jizo Sama, venerable protector by a certain riverside of Hades, where the ghost children play at massing pebbles!

Every night I watched one Jizo's idol in a neighboring temple yard, I remember, through the window of my home. Didn't I see in my imagination his mighty sleeves screening the dead children in the tragic scene with the demons chasing them? I heard the song of the children—poor dead dears!—sounding from a hundred thousand billion miles away:

> *"I recollect Mama, setting one pebble,*
> *My dear papa with my second. . ."*

I used to go to my bed when O Jizo Sama's lanterns passed way,—when all the ghost children must have gone to bed,—when Silence reigned over our world and one other world of Darkness.

Naughty Cissy spilled her coffee over his honorable head.

Alas! his one arm was off.

I suddenly felt as if I myself were a curio dug up from the dust of ancient ruin and exposed for a show like the armless O Jizo San.

My little mind soon rebelled, however, exclaiming that I will prove how I can hold water, although I may be a hand-broken Japanese mug.

You shall see, my Meriken Sama.

Letter VII

If my grandfather were alive!

My fancy's eyes can see the satisfaction that would beam from his face on hearing of my rising at seven in the morning.

I don't blame you, however, if you don't know how the sky looks at seven.

My grandfather defeated every opposition in naming me "Morning Glory," when a thousand other names—"Gossamer" and "Spring Moon" among them—were introduced. "Woman should be a morning glory, yes sir, rising before the sun," he did exclaim.

He was a terrorist, even believing that we women made our humble presence to serve "gentlemen" for the sake of blotting out the sins of our past lives.

If he could only know that I am not a failure, after all, in living up to the reputation of his morning glory! It is my grief always that I was born a bit too late. Isn't it really too bad?

I know he would be delighted to learn that I can be done with my hair within fifteen minutes every morning. How often did he say: "Sun will be set before seeing your hair perfect."

Matsuba San, it is my opinion that a servant, like a poet, is born.

You cannot study my family history without discovering that it is a singularly natural thing for me to have servant-blood in me. Didn't my ancestor perform the honorable hara-kiri from faithfulness to his lord?

(Some Americans say "Hara-kari." God knows what that means!)

I'm decidedly a better girl, I declare, since I learned how to serve.

Didn't I mend the broken china with glue that I found in a drawer?

I never pass by without picking up a pin from the floor-rugs.

How pleasing to see no carpet at Mrs Stuart-Dodge's! Carpet so cheaply neat! It is like a Japanese haori of hypocritical appearance. Is only a satirist to denounce the haori as a "poverty cover"?

The most unromantic part about Madam's rugs—Turkish or Russian, whatever they be—was that, Alas! a label attached to an edge of one rug in the parlour bounded out when my shoe rudely turned it.

$2,000!

Such an American millionaire!

Is Mr. Stuart-Dodge ready to sell it if any buyer comes long?

"Should I put the price on my Japanese kimono," I thought in laughter.

What use, I say, for the possession of honorable knowledge which I can't put into practice? Why should I disturb myself because of my fading memory of my school learning? Can $a + b = c$, a geometrical formula, be employed in dusting? I am mightily glad, dear Pine Leaf. My mind feels a deal lighter with no such stuff. What a simplification of me only cherishing a few ideas of how to manage a sweeper!

Certain dreamer anticipates a future household without any servant. Isn't parlor-maid the first on the list to be abolished when the scientific perfection of building shall do away with dust? It is my fortune to find myself just in time with Amerikey, is it not?

Madam said a nice thing about me.

I'm sure there was no "but" whatever,—what a reflective "but"!—without which her speech rarely terminates.

Don't I work hard?

Yesterday I was so completely worn out that I could not remind me of my cap when I hastened to my bed. How sadly I glance at my poor "crown" in the morning! Can you ever imagine what an awe-struck picture I was with my storm-tossed hair and my cap almost dropping? Worse than the ghost in "peony lantern!" Matsuba San, golden hair—O you lucky Meriken musume!—wouldn't look so bad in such a condition. Black hair! ("O hang it!" as the eternally lazy John might say.) It is the fate of the Jap girl that she should think of the shape of her hair even in her sleep. How awful!

I bought one dozen caps today to be ready for an accident.

Some of them are shaped like oyster-shells. Do you say I am crazy to wear such a thing?

Madam's speech is so slow, with each comma and semicolon in its proper place.

Her handling of the ever so courteous "You know" or "Don't you remember" is an infinite delight for the servant-girls.

Didn't I want to carry a tiny dictionary under my petticoats, fearing that the 'Merican millionaire's wife might use a tremendously long vocabulary?

Thank heavens! I found myself safe from any such danger.

I have discovered her own secret of popularity among us, Matsuba San. It is nothing but the correct calling of each girl by name.

Mr. Heine complained ever so much that eight out of ten of the letters sent to him misspelled his name. Uncle told him that he had no business to bear any infernally difficult first name. "Simplicity is the Keynote of America," Oji San pressed. The old poet laughed over his increasing stock of postage stamps since the enactment of his rule not to send any autograph but to one spelling his name correctly.

Are you suspicious of my ability, because I never mentioned his first name?

What humiliation we feel at being called by the wrong name!

I dare say that no American woman is learned in the art of growing old.

"Madam used to wear many jewels, even a fancy dress. But she has given them up since two years, when she admitted that she was growing old. She is now so simple like a lily," Marianna said.

I really think it about time for her to abandon the idea of being petted.

"To make a chaotic thing simple, to bring system out of confusion, to water and prune things until they blossom," were her work, as she declared.

It seems to me that the only noise she stirs is with her magnificent skirt, as she changes her seat in the drawing room while waiting for her carriage.

How mountainous she appears!

Don't I tremble lest she may swallow me up, you say?

Oh no, my girl!

Didn't I play with Oniwo Sama—the enormous idol guarding a temple gate—in my childhood?

But if she ever caught your M. G. in chitchat with Mr. Stuart-Dodge!

Does she approve her mighty millionaire cheapening himself to talk nonsense with such an inglorious maid?

Isn't it funny that we women always regard each other's talk as nonsense?

She would not pause a minute in discharging me if ever she saw me using my eyelashes to her husband wickedly.

(I never did, Matsuba San.)

Talkative old man!

He is ready any time to be reminiscent. He will bombard you with his episodes.

I am sure he often tells his love to his wife. He will not remark that there is another standard for man.

I am positive that he will not open his wife's letters, as a Japanese husband does.

It will be another matter for me to explore whether he was an editor in the struggling days of his youth. He bangs out his honorable "we" in a manly gentle voice. How I fear that he may tap my little back to give double value to his words!

Am I not cautious to keep a few feet apart from his for the occasion when I must hide under the table at sight of Madam?

How rapturous he was in hearing me say that the Hon. Harris (the first Meriken minister to the court of Yedo) was the greatest of the whole bunch!

Wasn't it grand of him not to let his faith be shaken a bit when his interpreter Housken was assassinated in the street, fortifying himself with the assurance that a people clean enough to take a bath twice a day cannot stay savage?

If he could see Japan of today!

"He was my uncle," Mr. Stuart-Dodge exclaimed.

Oh, my! Didn't I startle?

This is an honourable family of Amerikey, Pine Leaf, doubtless.

Presently he brought out a stuffy bundle of Mr. Harris' letters. It would be a deal more interesting if he kept them affectionately in his pocket.

Didn't I listen to his reading?

I neatly slipped away from him, however, when he was beginning to renew his honorable "That reminds me!"

Poor gentleman!

P. S.—All the boys around the house (including even Henry the old butler) said, so Nell whispered, that they wouldn't mind going to Hell for just a kiss with me.

What wretchedness!

I put the following paper on the kitchen door:

"To whom it may concern:

It is Morning Glory's sincere desire that you should stay in Heaven."

Letter VIII

27th.

"You must be a descendant of the pussy-cat who travelled to London to frighten a poor little mouse," I exclaimed, playfully twisting Zara's moustache.

Even a female one raises a moustache. The idea!

To be sure I kissed Zara!

Zara—such a saucy thing! What tremendous airs, as if she considered herself a whole business!

(Let me say here that all the girls ever admire Miss cissy for putting on no airs.)

Poor Sir Charles!

How facetious it sounds for a stable puppy with the homeliest nose imaginable!

Zara boxed Charles's ear painfully when he paid his homage yesterday. She even jeered over his degeneracy in having his tail cut, when he gently retired. He bore up bravely, however, like a 'Merican gent whose proposal only brings laughter.

Today I saw Sir Charles passing by the house on his way to the stable without one glance this way, and with a face straight as a Wall street broker's.

Poor doggie!

What an awful Zara! She visited the stable with an indifferent air since morning, and took up her scandalous flirtation with the horses. Where was Charles then, I wonder? I am told her favorite horse is Mr. Mikado.

Miss Cecilia went riding on the Mikado's back a while ago. How dashing she looked, my Pine Leaf!

Didn't I promise myself to win Zara's love?

One never can woo a cat after the style of the Conqueror as with a simple dog.

Who ever could believe in Zara?

Zara will arch delightfully, and purr round your skirt—when she is in the right humor—even rub herself ostentatiously against your feet to show her preference for your society. Alas, it was the fancy of a moment. You should not be surprised the next minute to see her pretending to sleep.

Did you expect the wanton animal to spring upon your knee?

Oh, no, she will turn away serenely, looking as if she had never known you in her life. She will spend a considerable time at her toilet, and by and by, she will find herself in the library, lulled in sweet meditation. What ecstasy if she catches Miss Cissy's scented handkerchief upon the floor!

(Madam is so careful about her handkerchiefs and her lorgnette.)

Suppose Zara passes by me a moment later? Surely she will cry once or twice. How sad she would appear if I were not punctual in response!

I am told that she will be gone for a day or two sometimes, but returns with renewed vigot.

She keeps a sweetheart somewhere, to be certain.

What frivolity! Such selfishness!

Like M. G., you say?

Matsuba San, I silently admit the charge.

Didn't I tell you I was a poor victim of circumstances for which Japan—even our Emperor—is largely responsible?

Your trifling chum was born in the verily doubtful period of Meiji. It would be too harsh to examine my qualifications for respectability. What could you expect?

I often wonder—what if I should marry an American?

My daughter—fancy my having one!—should not go to bed till she could flirt with one dozen European lords at once, and write one book every day.

It is Zara's way to begin by exhibiting her dainty suck which whitens so as it shakes. Isn't it her special art?

Then she will present her head to be kissed to Mr. Stuart-Didge if there be no one more acceptable around—like a little girl half in awe.

It doesn't take a minute for her to grow bold to jump upon the Louis XIV chair (Mind you, Pine Leaf, everything in the drawing room is after that XIV) and endeavour to place herself behind your back.

The young lady will not speak with you for a week, so Marianna says, if you ever exclaim "Scamp!"

Zara fills an important role for Miss Cissy, without which her Friday—"day at home"—would be a flat failure.

Who can blame a girl's occasional silence? Silence, however, is considered more calamitous than a cry in the Meriken drawing room. Her "Look at Zara! Isn't she lovely?" comes in appropriately. The whole company are glad of the rescue.

Whenever Zara is mentioned in their chat, she will cast a glance or two of delight, and even make a few remark which are no doubt equivalent to "So kind of you to say so!" She will retire gracefully on seeing the sandwiches and tea brought in, not forgetting to leave a word like "Hope for you a delightful time!"

It was two months ago that Miss Cissy found two kittens in a basket by her door when she returned late from the opera. A bowl of milk—not skimmilk, the family never uses it—was placed before them when she carried them in to her bed chamber. "My darlings, you must learn manners," she exclaimed, seeing them trample right into the bowl. She wiped their tiny feet, and let them sleep in her papa's boots. She was perfectly charmed in the morning, when one of them demonstrated her frolicsomeness by rushing against the curtain with a great show of excitement, while the other was satisfying her curiousity by peeping into half-open drawer.

The educated Ann named them Zara and Selima, after Horace Walpole's two dears. She would not for the world miss a chance of displaying her erudition.

"Zara, you saved my life," Miss Cissy said when she recovered from her illness. Doubtless Zara's acrobatic entertainment lightened the burden of her confinement in bed. There is today a belief that she wasn't ill at all, but just having sport to see how she could stir the house. Wicked girl! One morning she was striking her piano in her nightgown, having so slipped from bed. How dumbfounded she was, Nell told me, to see her doctor behind her! "You are all right, heh, ha," the doctor exclaimed sardonically.

Zara's reigning popularity was assured when she expressed her heroism by killing a mouse. Miss Cissy almost cried, they say, in her enthusiasm when Zara carried the dead in her mouth all over the house for inspection.

Miss Cissy would have put an Ad. in the paper for a little girl to amuse Zara when she was in poor health, if Mr. Stuart-Dodge hadn't objected to such foolishness, even reasoning with her that a cat had little liking for noisy children.

Once she took Zara to church, putting her in her large silver bag. She exclaimed "My sweet Christian puss," seeing her behaviour during the service.

If only she were not so irresponsible!

Poor Selima disappeared one day.

"Where is poor Selima now?" Miss Cissy would say sadly, as she was feeding Zara her dinner.

My God! Did she die? How I shuddered when Marianna betrayed the secret!

The second man, who left a while ago, took Selima up to his room. Eternally mischievous Selima jumped up to the open window. Alas, there was no screen! Poor thing! She dropped to the ground from three stories high.

John buried her one moon evening.

It is the educated Ann's everlasting grief that she made the mistake of giving her such an ill-fated name, as you know Walpole's Selima did drown herself in a tub, being tempted by a goldfish.

Shall I emulate the poet Gray by immortalising Meriken Selima's memory, I wonder?

What if Miss Cissy should ever hear of it?

MRS. STUART-DODGE ASSURED ME OF HER indifference as to what I wear on my day out (that is every Wednesday),—even if 1 put on my Japanese kimono.

Dear beautifully outlandish dress!

Why should she be against my red silk stockings if they smell sweet?

(She is so fastidious. She presents herself as clean as a silver tureen. Henry cleans all the silver every Monday.)

I sent an express man to Mr. Consul's for my trunk.

Oya, ma, where's the key?

Did I put it within? It would be fatal if so.

I called a locksmith.

He was surprised at observing such a gorgeous affair when he opened it.

I feared at once that he might tell the other girls. How could such be a reasonable equipment for a servant!

I kissed him, making him promise not to disclose what he saw.

My dear girl, I did honestly, honestly.

I wasn't a bit afraid, as he was such a young fellow.

I cannot find any clew, however, to judging Meriken people's age, at all.

I was awfully disgusted on account of my ignorance of packing my trunk.

Look! All my dresses were jammed sadly.

What? Did my toothpowder ruin my best waist?

What business had you to put in such a thing, Morning Glory?

Ara, ara!

"Your fellow is waiting by the kitchen door, Morning Glory. He's not a bad chap. He must be stuck on you tremendously," Marianna whispered me at evening.

Oya!

The blushing locksmith begged me to join him for a walk.

Matsuba, what do you imagine I said? "O sonny, be good boy, go home and sleep!"

Another kiss?

"Come back again when your moustache has sprouted," I exclaimed.

You can fancy how uninteresting to kiss any face smooth as O Binzuru!

Letter IX

Matsuba San,—

No servant in New York is looked upon as of legitimate standing if she can't sing "just Because She Made Dem Goo-Goo Eyes."

Why shouldn't we delight in the coon song?

I'm told that the big President of America is just crazy over singing "A Hot Time in the Old Town Tonight," when he is tired of discussing the Filipino question.

What a disgrace it would be in Japan if the mighty premier ever sang a dodoitsu in the cabinet!

Jolly America!

Nell promised to give me a lesson or two in the "Goo-Goo Eyes."

What do you suppose goo-goo eyes may be, Pine Leaf?

It is my honorable Nell's opinion that Love should begin with the "Goo-goo Eyes."

You know the Japanese eyes "glaring at the bamboo bush of a neighboring temple," don't you?

I laughed so much at the thought of casting a few 'Merican goo-goo eyes over the "Big Buddha" of Kamakura.

What would that immense idol (isn't his face ten feet long?) think of me!

Poor Nell sadly confided to me that she has been having bad luck ever since she left her last place for the family's sake, where her "beauty" created a furor among the young gentlemen, who were ready even to elope with her. Her goo-goo eyes are not effective recently, I fancy. What a pity! She doesn't worry, she says, as she still has a few young fellows in hand.

Henry says it is a sure mistake for Nell to flirt with so many fellows at once if she means to get married. "Why can't you wait until you have a baby?" he exclaimed. It is probable that the world will overlook your offence after two years of marriage in Amerikey if you do allow one to make love to you.

Isn't it terrible for her to write a letter to a stranger hyperbolizing her looks?

Where does she send it, I wonder?

Today she complained of her poor stock of rhetoric.

When I began thus: "My luxuriant hair curls on my head, sir, like a cloud. Your next question should be about my figure. It is slender as the branch of a willow tree," she exclaimed:

"Great Scot!"

Sometimes she says "Dickens!"

Does she mean the names of the famous writers?

Matsuba San, I think it wouldn't be a bad idea to popularize the great names of Japan for use as exclamations.

Mary said one day to Nell: "That's all very well, Nell, that you are clever enough to swear in seven languages, but I'm so sorry that you can't pray even in one."

Does she swear?

I have often heard her saying "Nit." My dictionary was not able to explain what it means. What is her "blankety-blank-blank" for heaven's sake?

I don't mind admitting that she is a bright girl, since she is able to tell which is a love letter from a glance over the envelopes of Miss Cissy's letters.

Can you imagine what a fuss those servant girls make over their letters?

When they hear the post-man's whistle in the morning—what a happy tune!—they will silently gather around the side-door. Some girl will even attempt to rise early and steal some flowers from the dining room table for her compliment to him. He will be rewarded with a few gentle taps on his cheek if he brings a big bunch.

But what if he has none for them?

Just watch the postman!

He will steal to the house quietly as a snail, and drop the other mail through a hole in the door, to avoid their reproaches.

The girls are expecting a marriage-offer, undoubtedly, without knowing from where it may come. They are mighty dreamers, like the poets.

(One of the honorable properties of a servant girl seems to be "Napoleon's Oraculum." I never saw any like them for dreaming so plenteously at night. They will trade their dreams at the table, and ask to see the book, presently.)

Lucinda was vehement this morning in saying: "How mean not to leave my letters! I am positive he has mine from dear Stockholm in his bag. Look at a thousand letters he carries! Not one for me among them? How can I believe it!"

Poor, poor Lucinda!

The educated Ann wouldn't cheapen herself so for the world, remaining divinely seated in her sewing room,—surely with her "soul" soaring into Poesy.

Isn't she hiding her book of poems in her basket?

How she would scorn the idea of hastening to send forth her poems to posterity, if I should ever inquire whether she ever put any in the hands of a publisher!

She unlocked the door of her mystery, however, with the following lines written upon "The Boxers' Yielding in China."

> *"And now that the struggle is done,*
> *Over and ended and past,*
> *(Fate so willed it) we must*
> *Travel together the road,*
> *And travel as comrades shall we."*

Tat, tat, Matsuba, don't be too quick with your pungent criticism!

Don't you know that stupidity at the start prophesies brilliancy in the middle?

Mary is always ready to declare "Nearer My God To Thee" the best poem in the world. And the second best, in her judgement, is "The World is Love, Every Day is Sunday," which was printed in the Avon Herald. The Herald, she assures me, never publishes poor stuff. And Avon, though the map cannot point to it, is the nicest spot on the face of the earth, so she said.

Ann appeared to me far greater when she told me that she had once passed over the bridge upon which Emerson wrote:

> *"Here once the embattled farmers stood,*
> *And fired the shot heard round the world."*

Will she ever permit me to write in her book of autographs, I wonder?

The girls cannot rest at all, they innocently confess, when they do not talk.

How funny, Pine Leaf!

When I went down to the kitchen ("Court Room" the butler calls it) this afternoon, I observed Mary in her habitual pose in one corner, terribly complaining of the degeneracy of modern girls.

Nell made a hit with her trip-to-heaven dream. (Another entertainment of hers is the occasional recitation of a chapter from the Bible.)

Poor Lucinda looked awfully sad from her failure to create any impression with her boast of having seen the Passion Play at Oberammergau.

Do you know where that is, Matsuba San?

"The gentleman who took the part of Christ was so handsome like Billy," she muttered.

"Billy"—a policeman—is her lover.

Did you ever think to risk so much in taking in such a giant as your sweet heart?

"Ack, ja!" she exclaimed, slipping pitifully.

She went out afterward. It wouldn't be any wonder if she asks every postman she comes across for her mail from Stockholm.

It is well understood that Theresa is gratifying her appetite for her daily nap, as she can't alter her programme from the one she fixed upon at a certain Parisian Countess'.

Sweet afternoon doze!

I'm glad to take it, if it doesn't betray the hereditary sluggishness of old Japan.

Theresa's egg must be boiled three minutes. Her digestion would be spoiled at once if it were more or less than that. Her fancy must be pleased above everything. "I must live like a lady, though I am a maid," was her proclamation.

She carries down her own tea-pot every morning for her own use.

The cord of good feeling between Mary and Theresa has been cut.

Theresa forgot to greet Mary with "Good Morning" two days ago.

Mary's attitude is that she will not condescend to any European imigrant.

We are looking for a serious fight, Pine Leaf.

Isn't that awful?

Did you ever eat codfish, Matsuba?

I thought no one expect Chinee would eat such a sort of thing.

Nell is positive in saying that she can live on codfish for one year and potatoes for another.

Must I learn to devour to be regarded as a servant girl?

The first question of those girls is always "Are you a Catholic?"

Do you call me silly if I tell you that I did order one scapular?

I was afraid a rosary might be too demonstrative.

I really wonder if you know what the S.A.G. at the corner of this envelope means.

Yours,
Morning Glory.

P. S.—I went through every room at Mrs. Stuart-Dodge's today.

The funniest thing I noticed is that some old calendar is hanging in every one.

What does that mean?

Matsuba, those rich people are awfully sentimental, you know.

Madam likes to cry over the old calendars, perhaps, like a certain poet who wrote upon "The Passing Century:"

> *"How shall we comfort the dying year?*
> *His hands are clammy, his pulse beats low."*

2nd P. S.—Nell told me as the secret of secrets that the old gentleman is busy with the revision of a book of Hymns.

So many a secret is hovering around here, Pine Leaf.

I am glad it is not a book of grammar.

Letter X

DEAREST PINE LEAF:

The dinner gong had been struck some time.

There's nothing more displeasing to Madam than the punctual announcement of dinner. Who talks of 'Merican accuracy?

O Matsuba, did you ever dream that such a Japanese gong, cast out from service in a temple, could fill another place in a Meriken household?

Won't you take up the work of sending a circular to every village urging that any old thing be sent to Amerikey?

The more useless the thing the more costly it becomes.

There's no surprise in seeing M. G. gracefully passing as a maid.

I dread the sad sound of a gong, since I can't think of it without recalling the chapter of "Tomorrow we shall turn to white skeleton," which my grandpapa used to read facing the idol.

I cover my ears with my hands when the gong rings, Pine Leaf.

How does it sound to Meriken San? Does it incite their appetite, I wonder?

Mary bitterly complained of the family's slowness in coming to dinner. She was adding water into the soup in the pan every two minutes.

(Mary's kettle upon the stove is always empty, Henry said. Cook careless with not water! Think of it!)

"It's no wonder if I can't get married while I work here. I'm missing my engagement with my fellow tonight. Isn't it too bad? My work won't be done before nine," Mary exclaimed.

That a thing has two sides is my present discovery. I was wrong in making my customary delay.

Poor Mary homely like George Elliot!

It is superfluous to say that cook and authoress are the only homely ones in Amerikey.

Is that why I am afraid to come out as a writer?

Did I tell you that "! !" or "? ?" will be the title for my book, if I ever should publish one? Jap girl is a little creature crammed with all sorts of exclamation and questions, you know.

There is nothing more commonplace than having a thing so simple to make the others understand at once.

Dear ever so shy cockroaches!

I wouldn't believe the Stuart-Dodges an old family if they did not put in an appearance.

"Didn't I feed you with olive oil, my honorable ones in black swallowtail?" I said.

(What an eternally changeless gentleman's dress! How frivolous is woman's!)

Henry showed me how to make a mayonnaise sauce.

It's a secret. I will not disclose it to you just yet, my dear girl.

By the way, how is your lettuce—"tiny leaf" as you call it—in the backyard growing?

Will you greet my return by presenting me with the choicest leaves of them?

Nothing could be more appropriate for a girl. Meriken girl will prefer death, surely, than to be without it.

I will mix a French dressing.

Matsuba San, to learn it is worth a journey to Amerikey.

What a pungency like a Spring breeze at dawn!

I am glad there is no flea here.

Who said that Japan is the country of fleas and jinrikisha men?

But I miss the mosquitoes in Amerikey.

How delightful it was to lie in a mosquito net, admiring the moonlight!

The four candelabra with the four candles in each were lighted in the dining room. You shall be conveyed away into a flowery dale by the voiceless song of the angels upon the ceiling. Behold the decoration, my Pine Leaf!

How often I drop the vegetable spoon upon the floor!

"Lady should be first, Morning Glory," Madam will say, whenever I begin by serving Mr. Stuart-Dodge.

What an impatient gentleman for the potatoes!

I'm so pleased not to see any mashed potatoes. What mustiness!

How could I think of giving anything to a daughter before her honorable papa has been helped.

Certainly Confucius should be blamed, not M. G., I tell you.

What a relief to find that any naughtiness of a maid in the pantry is beyond criticism, as with a lady in her dressing room!

Don't I steal a taste?

Matsuba, I shouldn't risk my reputation telling you such a thing.

It was last night that Henry wished me to wipe a vichy bottle. My goodness! 'Merican bottle is tricky as an elephant's trunk, do you know that? Did I push the handle? I was a pitiful show with my face spluttered by the water from the bottle. I ran upstairs to my room. I couldn't appear again till the dinner was over. Didn't I take a time to change my dress?

Henry goodnatured never scolding me!

(Madam cannot bear to see any carelessness with regard to the pantry indicator. The white tongue showing the bell's position should be raised up promptly, whenever I saw it dropped, Henry said. He was mighty glad that Madam didn't bother whith his work any more, since the day when she broke a dozen glasses—$5.00 apiece—intruding herself at the cleaning.)

I am trying, however, to keep at a distance from him, fearing he may put me in the uncomfortable position of having to listen to his own story.

I know, Pine Leaf, such a smiling old fellow always hides a contribution-book in his inside pocket like a Jap priest.

Poor fellow!

He would look better with a moustache. How sad that butler and coachman are forbidden it!

I fancied that Mr. Stuart-Dodge was loitering over his comic weekly.

Dear paper!

There a Plato appears as a circus clown in wanton garb.

I decided to present Uncle with one year's subscription. Wouldn't it be the best education for his after-dinner speech?

The lantern light of the conservatory adjoining the dining room had gone out, when the family finally sat down to dinner.

Dick takes care of the conservatory, saying that it demands plenteous care as the price of its smile (as with a woman, he might add).

Dick's bald head bears an eminent resemblance to that of Verlaine. Didn't you hear of the French poet, a mixture of god and devil?

He may have some poetry in him, too, that Dick. He was enraptured one day Miss Cissy's "Pretty Maiden," and couldn't help exclaiming:

"That's Shakespeare!"

At table Mr. Stuart-Dodge grieved upon modern people's disregard of fact.

(What will he say if he ever comes to a thorough knowledge of Morning Glory?)

Madam was so sorry that she could not find time to read David Copperfield again.

It was her impression that the color of Mrs. S——'s drawing room wall failed to hermonize perfectly with the furniture.

How hard Miss Cissy pleaded with Madam for a regular old-fashioned bread pudding, as she puts it.

Madam gave her daughter a few points on "How to be Popular in Society."

She remarks often on something about "400." Why not five hundred? I should like to know really.

P. S.—Decidedly one advantage of being a servant girl, Matsuba, is that no one will grow inquisitive on seeing you to ask how you like America.

What a nuisance, I always declared, to shake hands with one on being introduced!

Such a horrid sensation of being held by a hairy hand!

I'm perfectly free from it now.

"If you don't tell the other girls, there's no use to love a fellow," is Nell's idea.

All the girls are wild in telling about their "beaux."

Isn't it a pity that they are so awfully ready to let it be known whom they love?

Letter XI

Sweet Matsuba,

I dreamed the following dream:

Didn't I sail on the ocean, singing of my return to Japan? Didn't I?

There's nothing essier than a sail in a dream, Pine Leaf.

Sea-sick?

At last the sapphire sky revealed a white dome, extraordinary as if a home of God.

What rapture I had finding it nothing but my honorable Fuji Yama!

Suddenly to my visionary eyes my thousand Japanese comrades appeared by the mountainside. Were you among them? Most undoubtedly. The beautiful lanterns were nodding above their heads. A hundred cherry-blossoms laughed and laughed behind them.

"Okaeri asobashita, Morning Glory San! Honorable coming back!" they all cried out at once.

What were the gifts I brought for you, anyhow?

Isn't it too bad I have forgotten them all?

By and by, my steamer stole into Yokohama bay.

Didn't I hear already the "Pan, pan, pan!" of a tobacco pipe knocking the edge of a smoking box for the ashes? Listen! What an affectionate "Tap, tap, tap!" of bare feet upon the floor shiny as a lacquered tray!

Such a fantastically crooked pine tree so nicely bowed, seeing me from the Love Goddess Headland.

Did you ever see any tree's welcoming bow, I wonder?

My beloved cicadas whizzed most triumphantly by.

"Arigataya! Land of shamisen and Buddha idol, again!" I exclaimed.

Finally my steamer anchored.

What monkey-faced savages were those jinrikisha men! They pulled wildly at my skirt, entreating my honorable ride. My poor legs—Oh dear!—were thrown into exhibition. How bitterly they quarrelled for the possession of me!

A moment later I was placed in one carriage turned toward my home.

I rode 'long a street, where such a smothering smell overflowed.

It was evening, to be sure.

The people were cooking supper, evidently. Frying sea-weed, I said? Stewing lotos-roots, perhaps. I had lost all my memory of Japanese fare.

I laughed to think how funny it would be if I had to live on bamboo leaves only.

My vehicle ran through the crowd of ghostly children.

They were singing aloud with their flat noses toward the sky. One big Buddha idol looked at me suspiciously, from behind the gate of a temple, when my jinrikisha man turned the street. What indignation I felt at not being recognized as Morning Glory!

Behold! the sky changed at once into a looking glass.

Oya, ma, I saw myself heavily covered with golden hair.

Wasn't I frightened to see my body enlarged? Look at my feet growing so terribly! Where were my tiny ones of yesterday?

O Matsuba, I felt as if I were running on the roofs, the Japanese houses had become so ridiculously low.

"Have I really turned to a Meriken girl? Oh, what a shame! What will my mama say?" I fancied her terrified eye flung upon me.

I cried. How I cried!

"ARE YOU SICK, MORNING GLORY? Eight o'clock already!" Nell was striking on my door.

My God!

I was sweating awfully from such a dream.

What does it mean?

Had my hair turned to golden hue?

I kissed my feet, seeing no change in them. How glad I was, Pine Leaf!

(It was a perfect shame to have such long toe-nails. I hadn't trimmed them for many a month. Such negligence!)

I felt all right upon the girls' assurance that I was the self-same M. G.

But what shall I do if I look an American girl to my mother when I return to Japan?

I mistrust that my little charm which I lost while on the ocean may work a dirty trick upon me.

Dear Matsuba, will you make a hundred-time pilgrimage to one popular god to keep me secure from any harm?

Don't forget an oblation of the best wine, my girlie!

Even the god will be delighted to be tipsy once in a while, you know.

P. S.—Mr. Stuart-Dodge left the library from fatigue in his reading.

Wasn't I disappointed to find his book neither Maeterlinck nor Ibsen?

I don't worry a bit about my total lack of their acquaintance, because I am told that the demand for them is ebbing.

What's coming next?

My Pine Leaf, I am so patient waiting for Confucius' day. I will show you then how easily I can take a leadership.

The library's shelves are occupied by the edition de luxe.

Don't insult them by asking whether their leaves are cut!

Authors are hopelessly degenerated in such an edition, like the stage general in a Japanese play, to whom a helmet is everything.

"I wouldn't mind even a book of poem, if illustrated. A book without a picture is as shocking as a house with no curtain," Miss Cissy would say, dropping into the library.

Suppose she plucks one book?

It is a settled thing that she will leave it somewhere before she goes upstaire.

Matsuba San, I found a key upon the table.

My hereditary curiosity was vivified at once. I ventured to imagine that the key might open one of those cases wherein I should not fail to discover the most wonderful book of the world.

Did I apply it?

Why, didn't I, Pine Leaf?

What did I find in the case?

"History of the Stuart-Dodge Family."

I was so glad to have my chance of exploring Mr. Stuart-Dodge's black cap of Dr.

Oya, ma, what?

It was merely a colonel's.

Poor Colonel Stuart-Dodge!

Letter XII

Look at Miss Cissy poking her nose into the flowers of the drawing room every morning!

What would our dear poet Kenko say if he saw her?

Didn't he satirize a girl at gaze with the cherry blossoms close beside her?

Certainly admiration from a distance is higher.

Miss Cissy's nose, however, is lovely, is it not?

I will not try to defend myself if someone says that Morning Glory could not stand Amerikey, because she was awfully jealous of her pretty girls, and so left for England.

(My beloved Matsuba, I will begin my new voyage pretty soon in fact.)

Meriken girls could be perfect, I should say, if they were a bit more regulated in their proportions.

Voila! (Doesn't it fit in her?—although I never know its meaning. Theresa often exclaims it.)

Aren't their honorable "below the waists" too improper in size?

Dick set three azalea plants in the drawing room, carrying them out from the green-house.

The sight of them revived in my mind a song that my maid used to sing:

> *"Satemo migotona Odawara tsutsuzi!*
> *Motowa, Hakoneno yamasodachi."*

(What a lovely Odawara azalea! She was bred originally at Hakone mountainside.)

Pine Leaf, wouldn't you lile to visit the Stuart-Dodges' green-house?

Let us not forget to bow to O Jizo Sama—you don't mind how long it be, do you?—as we pass by!

No, my Matsuba, we shan't spend a moment looking over the old china 'long the passageway.

What will you say when you see the bronze statue of a young botanist by the door, whose zealous fingers would not leave one petal untouched?

We will not miss the head gardiner's ancient smile of reception.

His manner of slightly bowing as he talks is awfully pleasing, don't you think?

It would be fun to count how many hairs he has, while he sleeps.

I can't help feeling quite nervous whenever I see him walking. His shoes—almost two feet long, Matsuba—are in such peril of sliding off from his feet with each step.

I cannot see why his spectacles are needed, if he must place them on the edge of his nose. Oh, very likely he wishes one or two ornaments for his face. Poor fellow!

(By the way, it is impossible to persuade Miss Cissy to take a French lesson without her glasses. I suppose she thinks she must at least appear studious.)

Isn't the gardiner's jumper a heavenly change from the Stuart-Dodge mode of dress?

Its delightful looseness is a protest of the countryside against the formalism of New York.

Could I try it on for even once? My patent-leather-tipped shoes would make a striking contrast with its sea-blue pants, doubtless.

"'Papa,' what is its honorable name?" I will say, pointing to an orchid.

(All the girls call him "Papa" playfully. He accepts it with a graceful ease. Dear man!)

What naughtiness! Aren't we delighted to vex him by asking the names of the orchids without a bit of necessity? It is whispered around, however, that hereafter the old man will not tell us their names except by Madam's order. It is verily nice once in a while to hear a tremendous name about one mile long. Its unintelligibility is part of our great satisfaction.

"Only botanical names here, girls! Do you fancy this is a common meadow where the buttercups grow?" he will exclaim if you ask why he does not call things by plain names.

Presently he will take you to "Cattleya Gaskelliana Alba"—heaven knows what it does mean!—and never fail in telling you that it is valued at $4,000.

He will even assure you that it is the only one in the whole city.

Isn't it remarkable that he is always ready to speak out the name and price of a thousand orchids?

It is of no use, Matsuba San, to quarrel with him over the floral superiority of orchids or violets. He considers the orchids as the only things deserving of his important attention.

"But, 'Papa,' no poet has written about orchids," I may venture.

"How could he when he couldn't see them? His information must have been restrained to cheap flowers. Those valuable orchids should be far beyond the reach of a poor poet," he will slap me back, his belief not stirring a bit.

What an apology!

"They are common things," he will keep repeating when he accompanies you to the parts where are roses and carnations. You shall even observe some sweat falling from his brow in his shame at bringing you before such an insignificant exhibition.

Aren't you glad you don't see any geraniums at Stuart-Dodges'?

Suddenly you shall be carried to the Orient! You shall certainly suspect that you are a victim of illusion.

Behold a hundred plants before you!

What a pitiful dwarfishness as if from the heavy grief of a thousand years! Such a sad mark of morbidness!

Deliver me!

The lotos flowers—what saintliness!—slowly shake out their white smile. Is it for some celectial joy?

The sun may creep in to stamp the shadows of fishes in a wodden pond. Gold fishes to be sure. What a supernatural grace in the shadows! What an undisturbed gesticulation of the fishes mocking the bustle of Greater New York!

"Papa" will request your signature by and by, presenting the "Visitor's Book."

Dear Pine Leaf, don't forget to write it down in Japanese!

Let us go back slowly along the passageway!

I cannot help hearing in my imagination the songs of wanton abandonment of the jolly drunkards—God bless them!—when I look at the shelves of mugs on both sides. Surely I see one with face distorted with laughter and sarcasm, whose song will be thus ended abruptly:

> *"If life were merchandise which men could buy,*
> *The rich would live, the poor alone would die."*

(The lines written on one of the mugs.)

Don't be scared, my dear girl, to see a bitter philosopher metamorphosed from the great collection of pepper boxes in the air!

Won't you hug our beloved O Jizo Sama, Matsuba?

I will shut my eyes for a while, if you don't mind. How can I bear the sight of a Japnese girl's awkwardness in kissing!

This evening was so terrible, Pine Leaf.

The fight broke at last between Theresa and Mary.

Marianna whistled around announcing that our supper would be half an hour earlier.

You bet, Theresa was excursioning to a fairy realm—perhaps to her Parisian countess'—in her afternoon nap.

She reged at seeing nothing upon the table when she came down.

She rushed toward the stove with her honorable tea-pot, when Mary objected to her taking the hot water.

Mary ran up stairs crying, and appealed to Madam against Theresa barbarity in pouring the boiling water over her arms.

"A Christian lady can't do other than discharge her," Mary declared afterward. She even whispered to me about Mrs. Stuart-Dodge's profound confidence in herself.

Theresa was summoned shortly and sentenced to leave the house.

Nell advised her not to forget to take her tea-pot.

Suspicious Lucinda watched all the time in fear she might steal her picture of Billy.

John hurried to the green-house for a bunch of "forget-me-nots."

Nell told us afterward as a great news, that it was not on account of Mary, at all. (I'm glad Mary wasn't there to hear it.) Madam makes her midnight inspection all over the house. She saw a white thing crawling into the kitchen a few nights ago. Alas, it was Theresa! She was enjoying her midnight supper. Madam didn't approve it, surely.

Letter XIII

April 1st.

Beloved Matsuba:

What a responsibility your little friend does feel when she locks the safe!

Oh, what if I should forget the combination before morning!

Safe, dear!

How many Japanese girls did ever come across one?

One grand safe is set in a hidden closet of the drawing room.

I am really tickled to death thinking whether M. G. 's heart be so mysterious that it has to be unlocked like the safe.

I often said that a boy's mind is like a Japanese "oseba akimasu"— "it-does-open-if-you-push-gate"—whose door is always ready for yawning. Haven't we girls full liberty to trample in?

What a shame it would be, however, if every boy kept a combination for opening a girl's heart!

By and by, Morning Glory will bring out a silver snuff-box from the safe.

Look, how solemn she is in carrying it!

Is it truly the Queen Victoria's honorable gift to the Hon. Mr. Harris in gratitude for his service in consumating the first treaty with Japan?

(By the way, I'm not a bit enthusiastic about sailing toward London. It would be too sad to see dear fat "Mother" no more.)

O Pine Leaf, you must not be slow in hiding yourself behind the drapery when Mr. Stuart-Dodge passes by! He is awfully clever in pulling you in to listen to the romance of the snuff-box.

Don't forget to show him a few grimaces for your silent insistence on his shortening his story when he begins, "Let me start from the beginning!"

How dramatic he is when he tells how its darkest hour was when it was thrown in a pawnshop!

You must say something presently about being occupied. If not? He will ask you to come up to an attic to look over the honorable effigies (Ohina Sama) sent from Japan by Mr. Harris, many a year ago, in honor of his dead sister.

His description of the Japanese dolls' festival of the third of March is preferable to his reminiscences of his sister, no doubt.

But you might say that you know all about that? He will flash his indignation. "Oh, no, little thing like you—although you be Japanese—does know nothing," he will declare.

The family is wild about the Japanese, so Marianna always says.

There is no smallest doubt about it, Matsuba.

Do you know why?

The mystery was cleared today.

Listen! It is plainly from curiousity, not from appreciation of the worth of Japanese. What a shame!

You would pity M. G. if you heard that she was hired just for a show. The fortunate part about me is that it was not for a dime museum.

"Morning Glory, your speech is too perfect for Japanese. How I wish you could speak broken English like an actress in a Japanese play," Madam exclaimed.

How disgusted I was, you can imagine!

Alas, deficiency is the verily chief motive of the Japanese fad in Amerikey!

Where is 'Merican practicality?

I thought afterward that I wouldn't mind learning pigeon English if Madam would raise my wages.

You bet she would prize me dearer if I had only one eye large like a lantern.

Must I hop like a sparrow in the drawingroom? I almost decided to use less English, filling in with much quantity of hashed Japanese.

I am sorry I really can't succeed in making me a puppet like a Jap heroine in Meriken story, who titters "Ahé, hé, hé!" endlessly.

Imagine, dear Matsuba, what a mighty business it would mean if we should form a "Servant Girl Immigration Co."

Suppose we let the girls from Kazusa—is it not the country noted for O San Don?—march along Broadway? What a music from their wooden clogs! They must not wear any hat. A hand-wipe (tenugui) shall wind their heads, perhaps half their faces also. It will be the honorable flower-viewing style. For heaven's sake, don't let them hide their hana kanzashi under the tenugui! The design upon it should be the picture of the wealth god sitting on the rice-sacks. What an omen!

The rich American people will bid the highest price for their possession.

You can rest assured that they will not wait a minute to engage an interpreter for the girls, that is if they don't catch on to the "Ing'lis."

"What?" I exclaimed, when Nell asked me earnestly whether I was a true Jap.

All the girls declared, she said, that my nose wasn't Japanese. That I may be a Jewess masquerading as a Jap was their suspicion.

Wasn't Rebecca in Ivanhoe pretty?

But I should like to stay as a musume, since she may prove a better possibility for romance than a "Christ-Killer." (Permit me to use Mary's word.)

I went up and down the back-stairs, singing a song.

Will the Japanese tinkle vindicate me?

FOR THE LAST TWO HOURS Mrs. Professional Beauty of Society,—as the girls call her,—kept unfolding her art of compliment in the drawing room.

I know she is carrying a book of etiquette under her stocking.

Her "How lovely" must be the beginning, of course. "Charming indeed" cannot but be the ending.

Her admiration is started, say, with the picture of Cupid. "What a likeness to your beautiful Cissy!" she will exclaim.

(Marianna said Lucinda gained such favor with Mr. Stuart-Dodge from her praising of Cupid. She even advised me to follow the same track. Isn't it too bad I have been given no chance yet?)

A moment ago Mrs. P. B. declared that Madam's sandwiches were perfectly wonderful.

How could she miss admiring Madam's dress!

How astonished she was, she said, that her friends (mentioning Nancy, Polly, Nol, and Jess) got married to such dunces!

Presently she will come round to her "Darling Jack."

What a poor husband Jack, I thought.

He must find his satisfaction in a purple smoking jacket, when he is left alone at home. He must be grateful indeed, that she is his better half. He must be wide-awake for chances to speak about it in the press.

He should be like a chin koro doggie loitering in his aimless sort of way on the outskirts of the crowd that surrounds his wife patiently waiting for her cloak to be thrown.

"Husband of Mrs. P. B." he will say surely if you ask. O Matsuba, not a Mr.!

It is one of the most touching things imaginable to listen to her talking over his likes, his dislikes, and above all, of their mutual adoration.

Isn't she killing?

(Thus Miss Cissy might exclaim.)

Suppose Mr. Stuart-Dodge comes back from his drive?

He will not let the horses gallop, begging them rather to trot to the tune of "God save the King." Don't you know, Pine Leaf, that every New Yorker turns to an Englishman when he becomes rich?

Does Mr. Stuart-Dodge sniff Madam's company from the outside?

He will approach the stable as calmly as a ship sails into haven. He will bid adieu to his Black Fancy and Nut-Brown Maid. He never forgets to tap the noses of the horses, and even to examine their shoes like a professional.

How fastidious he is, the stableman says, in selecting the horses which he drives! By the way, he keeps more than fifteen. (Sitting behind the trotters is the only delight he has, so Mr. Stuart-Dodge says. Poor gentleman! We girls are awfully glad it is not his singing.)

He never makes any fuss at table whatever. Isn't it a sure mark of the "Self-Made Man?"

He greets a roast beef if it appears every day through the week. How bourgeois is the roast beef,—like a Japanese broiled eel! Dear unagimeshi! He will be awfully pleased if the eggs are from the country.

He has nothing to complain of, Henry said, so long as the side-door is tight, and nobody touches his wine bottle.

And one more thing! His high hat should be brushed carefully on Sunday.

Isn't it funny Henry has never seen where he keeps his claret?

How could he dare to ring the front door bell when it might stir the company! He will fist on the side-door apologetically.

You will see him shortly climbing the stairs.

I wish, Matsuba, he would give a few ideas to Uncle on how to leave woman alone.

Uncle could be a remarkable bore, but nothing else, you know.

Letter XIV

"An honorable fox wedding feast must be going on somewhere."

Look, how prankishly the sun-flashes play at hide-and-seek with the shower!

You know the Japanese saying on such a day.

Do you remember, Matsuba San, how many a year ago we used to play at a marriage ceremony? It was you, dear, who took the part of a bridegroom. I know you sang:

> *"Matsuni naritaya, Arimano matsuni,*
> *Tsutani dakarete netegozaru!"*

(I would like to be the pine-tree—Arima's pine tree. He sleeps in the ivy's arms, he!)

Didn't I put my arms around you? We pretended to sleep as husband and wife, didn't we?

O Pine Leaf, if you were here with me today!

Couldn't I take you in as a Charley?

A Charley is as necessary to an American household as a Taro to a Japanese one. The stable dog has to fill the gap at the Stuart-Dodge's.

Does it sound to you like a family idiot?

Any dictionary will assure you that the name signifies "manliness."

You would be stunned to see Mrs. Stuart-Dodge's bed, such a pompous affair!

I wish I could lay me down in it for even one night.

It is far greater than Napoleon's bed which I saw at the Golden Gate Park museum in Frisco.

A bureau stands in one corner of Madam's room. A bureau without any drawer! Just think! A pillow case will promptly peep out when you tug it a little bit. You would be quick to take Madam for a sinner if the chambermaid didn't explain that it was only a folding bed. Did you fancy she was keeping a secret sleeping place?

O wicked Matsuba!

What little wretches we are!

"Is it any shame to stay a bed in the daytime, you hypocrite?" I said, looking severely upon the folding bed.

Let me tell you that in Madam's dressing room there is a picture "The Light of the Harem." If it were not so dark you would "drop your liver" to find yourself on a divan, facing a girl who reclines attended by her slaves, and who wears a large ear-ring like the halo of an idol.

Shall I turn an electric light?

There on the dressing table you will see a picture of a boy.

Poor Master Ned!

Marianna said that Madam was not so passionate in church-going before his death.

Is there any place beside a prie-dieu where the egoism of sorrow could sleep?

Madam will excuse your any fault if it is linked with religion.

"Tell Madam, Henry, that I was reading the Bible, if she asks why I was late," said Mary one morning.

She even defended her serving of baked apples for luncheon dessert five days in succession by saying "Bishop Gregory had them every day for two weeks."

A door beside the picture will take you into a room where hangs Madam's gown. What care I for such a black affair!

You can't help suspecting that her first husband—if she had another—was a shoe-merchant, when you see a hundred shoes spread before you.

Is she not one "who will keep even an evening funeral, thinking it may turn to something after ten years," as Japanese say?

"The Duchess" (manicure you know) came to file Madam's nails a while ago.

Madam will push the button for her horses when her nails are in order.

Presently the inspiring clear music of the hoofs will quicken towards the front door.

O Matsuba, just look at the coachman! Isn't he worth seeing?

How solemn he is!

No stone idol could beat him for gravity.

It is said the first qualification for a coachman is a serious face. Why not use a dummy, since the 'Merican horses are so learned where to go?

Once all the servant girls had a contest to see which could bring him to a smile. Did any succeed, you say? No, Pine Leaf, not one!

Then they dubbed him "The wax-warks coachman of the Eden Musée."

I fancy he is afraid some oue may take a picture of him and so holds himself ready for such an encounter at any minute.

Poor coachman!

His mighty self-control wasn't a bit appreciated.

(Say! Wouldn't his picture make a splendid "Nerve Tonic" Ad.?)

You cannot help adoring him, when you come to realize his heavenly patience.

If Shaka Muni had been born in New York City I am sure he would never have gone into the deepest mountain to learn patience, but would have found a place as coachman instead.

You wonder if Madam's coachman can be so serene without being absorbed in a solution of the enigma of Life and Death which he carrying on in his mind.

"Philosopher, certainly!" I exclaimed.

"Meditations in a Coachman's Box" must be the title of his book. Has he reached the 156th page, I wonder? Isn't that the most interesting time, when we have things half done?

Imagine him going out with Miss Cissy.

She will drop in at her friend's with an "It's great!" or some such exclamation. A few hours will soon pass while she is chattering about the play and the actors.

("It's pretty hard to keep a girl from geting stage-struck in New York City," Uncle once said. Is that so?)

By and by, she will quit her carriage again at a dry goods store. She will begin by hunting for her handkerchief, of course. Suddenly she will be startled by hearing her name from behind. Presently you will find her with her friend comfortably settled before the counter, talking over their plans for the summer. You will see their shoulders shrug when a saleswoman notifies them that the door is about to be shut.

But the coachman will not suffer a bit, not he, his whole soul being engrossed in the beginning of his new chapter.

Just as Madam got into her carriage today, a telegram arrived.

(Her carriage is a brougham today. Not such a ghastly one, mind you, Pine Leaf, as that of our ever so dear Marquis R—'s. I should like to buy one for him.)

"How stupid," Madam exclaimed, seeing that her telegram was hopelessly indistinct.

O Matsuba, I smile over my cleverness at every sort of mystification, but alas! not over my handwriting.

Yesterday I received a letter from the poet Heine.

What writing!

Did I keep his letter?

No, Pine Leaf, I returned it to his Heights with much thanks.

I tried it upside down, after a vain attempt to read it in the ordinary fashion.

"Poor Uncle!" I exclaimed this morning, when he sent a message begging me to come back to his hotel. He left Mr. Consul's three days ago.

He wrote me that he would come in a carriage, reaching Stuart-Dodge's at four o'clock.

Didn't I jump?

"He shan't ruin my adventure when things are just beginning to be interesting," I declared sternly.

Didn't I tell him that I would put Sir Charles on him, if he ever dared to come near the house?

Dear old man! If he should ever see the stable dog!

He has such a terrible idea that we women are really fit for nothing but for telling a lie, that Uncle! He actually showered me with telegrams and messages—to such a dangerous point that the girls were almost aroused to suspicion,—for the last few days, not believing my statement that I was safe.

Isn't he ridiculous asking whether he shall send a hairdresser?

I am so glad I didn't tell him about my arms hurting me. You can judge how ready he would be in sending a doctor.

I soon replied to his message, saying that I "had a nice thing to tell him" befor he should come in a carriage. "We will meet by the kitchen door at eight," I wrote him. He should whistle some gay Nigger tune by the back door, I said, if he was able. Did he ever learn any, I wonder? That's the proper way for the girls fellows to do, Matsuba. If he couldn't? I said that he should throw a stone against the gate.

Pine Leaf, I utterly forget to tell him not to come tn his frock-coat.

It was eight o'clock already.

Did I see any sign of him? No!

I felt nervous thinking of the possibility of his being arrested by a policeman ss a suspicious character.

"Uncle!" I exclaimed, when I saw one lighting his cigar. Alas! My uncle wore a stovepipe hat.

How glad he was to see me alive! Did I not even get a red cheek? He almost cried, dear Uncle!

I took him into a little room by the kitchen which is our reception room, you know. Poor Mr. Secretary of the biggest Company!

I brought a glass of milk and a piece of pie from the pantry, the customary treat of the girls for their company.

All the girls traversed the room in their fancy to see what sort of a fellow I had got.

Fellow?

Why! Uncle is a gentleman.

I know they were wondering whether he was a vaudeville artist No Japanese except a magician on the stage wears a silk hat in Amerikey.

Madam's sudden bell rang summoning me just as I exclaimed, "No, Uncle! I got to stay here one month at least. I must have my full wages," on being told that we were to sail on the eighteenth.

I heard with satisfaction of our new travelling companion.

(Minister at Washington.)

"Go, Uncle, be quick now! I will write you tomorrow," I pushed him out as I ran upstairs.

Poor Uncle, how dumbfounded he was!

All the girls were wild to hear someting about him.

"There's no question about it that he is the best gentleman ever stepped in this kitchen for last ten years," Marianna said.

Lucinda couldn't believe that Uncle's chain was real.

I took their breath away, telling them that he was stopping at the Waldorf-Astoria.

Oh, how interesting it was, Matsuba!

Didn't I leave the matter cleverly upon a perilous border?

Letter XV

"I like just such disorder,—orderly disorder, I should say, Mother. It seems as if I were trevelling. When are we going to Europe?" Miss Cissy will say, whenever Madam attempts to straighten the books upon the table on entering her daughter's room.

Does she read them all from the beginning to finis?

Wasn't I, Pine Leaf, the cleverest of the whole bunch in our school deys for skipping the dull pages of a book?

I should fancy that Merican girls might be far more adroit in such an art. But then, of course, they are not obliged to read them through, since they only got to say, "It's powerful!"

O Matsube, I often think that my future husband should be a sport with an immense passion for hunting or riding horseback.

Why, you ask?

I may have chances, you know, of exhibiting my mighty devotion when he shall fall from his horse and lay himself bleeding from a big cut in his back.

Not in his forehead, for Heaven's sake!

I begin to fear that no one apprehends my tenderness of heart.

Dear Cissy!

Undoubtedly she has the same ideal as I, since she hangs every sort of sportsman's picture on her wall

"What does that corner mean?" I exclaimed, seeing a pair of dirty shoes.

Once Madam declared they were worse than measles. Miss Cissy insisted with tears that she must keep them for remembrance of the good times she had with them. They were tennis shoes.

My Pine Leaf, did you ever hear about tennis, I wonder?

"The Corner of Souvenirs," as she calls it, is her delight.

It is Madam's eternal grief, I am told, that she made the mistake of sending her daughter to college (Miss Cissy spent a year at Smith), where she contracted such bad habits. Poor Madam! She is patiently waiting for her to get through with that stage.

I couldn't help suspecting that she had robbed the kitchen of a well-known poet living on a hillside, when I observed a broken golf stick tied with a worn-out towel.

Didn't I recall how Mr. Heine once said that his kitchen utensils were always missing when college girls invaded his home?

Oh, My Matsuba, can you think what a revelation it was when I found myself in her dressing room?

Didn't I throw my envious eyes upon "Paris" stamped upon each cover to twenty hat-boxes?

Paris! How romantic it does sound! What beauty it breathes!

To be sure I tried all the hats on me.

(All the family had gone out in tha carriage, promising that they would not return for some hours.)

Think, Pine Leaf, there are ten low-neck gowns!

How I wished I could try one of them for once in my life! Every one tempted me terribly.

"Certainly you can," Nell assured me, when I spilled my secret.

Sweet Nell girl! Didn't I kiss her?

I sadly looked over my dark arms as I sat before the mirror.

What a shame! My vaccination marks—six on each arm—appeared disgracefully,

How bitterly I condemned the Japanese health doctors, you can imagine!

The carriage stopped at the front door just as Nell had begun to powder my shoulders.

"My Lord!" we both cried.

I turned death-like, trembling in fear, when I heard Miss Cissy's gay voice humming. I put myself in a closet instantly.

A moment later, the door was opened.

There stood the young lady.

Matsuba, your frivolous chum cried and cried, laying hereself on the floor before Miss Cissy.

Nell told her the whole situation briefly.

Miss Cissy burst into laughter.

"That's all right, Morning Glory! Come, dear girl, finish your dressing! O Mother, hurry up-stairs! Mother, you will see how charming Morning Clory looks in my dress! Didn't I tell you she was the prettiest girl I ever saw? Mother!" she called after Madam.

You may be sure that M. G.'s face caught fire from such wretchedness.

Was Madam pleased?

Of course not.

How can she be different from any rich Japanese housewife who is glad to be disagreeable once in a while?

She was indignant, no doubt.

THE WHOLE EVENING I STRUGGLED for a chance to thank Miss Cissy and make her promise to defend me when Madam should proclaim that I was discharged.

Alas, no chance at all!

Miss Cissy rang after me for the quinine pills at nine.

The hall was dusky.

A white bare arm was thrust out from the door to receive them.

I held it tight, and kissed it to stamp my weighty confidence in herself.

"It was Madam's, my goodness! O Morning Glory!" I cried, feeling presently that it was not a young girl's.

When I came down the front stairway, the owl dreadfully grinned from the drawing room, disdaining my frivolity.

(I hated it since my first day, Matsuba.)

How could I sleep with such an awful feeling!

4th.

Mr. Stuart-Dodge could not escape being arrested, if in Japen, for bestowing such an august name upon his horse.

I'm glad for the horse wearing such a mighty distinction in Amerikey, however.

Mikado!

Wasn't I astonished, Matsuba San, to find Mikado no other than our dear "First Runner," once owned by our neighboring general Yamaji— "One-Eyed Dare-Devil"—as he was called in barbarous adoration?

Didn't we say that he went to search after his lost eye, when he died? What a bloody-faced pride in him! Didn't he pluck out his own eye at school by way of explaining to his comrade that he wasn't a bit of a coward?

Poor General died soon after seeing every glory in the China war.

His beloved "First Runner" was sold away to 'Hama.

We didn't hear about him afterward, did we?

How could we, when he was sheltered on Fifth Avenue!

Pine Leaf, there's no mistaking about him at all. The sure mark is his white patch on each leg,

There's no sadder sight than one who has only to ponder over his victorious past.

If "First Runner" had met with a worse lot!

He might now be pulling a water cart 'long a zigzag street, beaten by the driver every two minutes.

(Dear Matsuba, I think sometimes what will happen if I ever marry with such a horse-beater. Does he whip his wife in the same fashion? It might be interesting. But I wish he will not spit so terribly.)

How can I help feeling pity, however, to see my big warrior turned to a retainer for a young girl! What degradation!

Wasn't it he that neighed first "Ten Thousand Years for Our Empire" standing triumphantly upon the newly-taken Manjuyama fort, when the white canvas of a Chinese tent and the red banner turned to a Nippon flag, waving in the dawn-breeze?

Poor horse!

Who in the stable will listen to the story of his Chinese campaign?

The lucky part is that Miss Cissy is pretty. They will make a splendid show in the park, doubtless.

Dind't I pray that she will not lash him? Shall I hide all her whips?

"Well! well!" I exclaimed, when he stretched out his neck, certainly speaking, "Mightily glad to see you here, Morning Glory,—is it you, really?"

Can you imagine how he looked, Pine Leaf, with his affectionate eyes filled with tears?

Dear fellow!

"Shibarakudawa," I repeated, caressing his face.

How nervously he shook his ears from zeal to hear my Japanese!

The coachman suddenly appeared, saying, "You like horse, don't you?"

Did I ask him about his philosophical work?

Is he pessimist? No, he should be optimist, I think.

O Matsuba, I left the stable abruptly, fearing my fancy might be ruined.

Evening turns everything worse with me, you know.

Letter XVI

(M. G. misplaced the following letter in
Miss Matsuba's envelope.)

5th.

My sweet one:

You are really a little late in discovering that a girl is a deal cleverer than a gentleman.

Even a Japanese girl, you say?

Why not!

Poor Oscar San!

Let me tell you that your frankness pleased me hugely!

Am I vain?

Not at all, my lord!

Oscar, you should be a tiny idol painted in gold. I will not forget to paint its eyes blue. I wonder whether you can stay gently in my heart-temple locked in by my passion.

Would you like a vain woman, as a man in a story necessarily does?

Shall I endeavour to be one?

My papa always complained tremendously of my fancifulness.

Truly, sir, I have too much of it.

Isn't it risky to love such?

Imagine me meeting a young man (Oscar, what will his name be?) under the wistaria in Central Park! I am told that the park wistaria is lovely. Sweet fuji! How dear "under the wistaria" is to me, ever since I used to quarrel with my playmates upon our height! What a triumphant sensation I had whenever the flower touched my hair! What fun it was if it ever got entangled with my hanakanzashi!

Oscar, my young man will hypnotise me there certainly.

How interesting to fall a victim!

I don't mind the trouble of sending you the book of hypnotism. You should learn its secret by all means.

Shall I elope with my young man?

Don't you feel jealous?

One fault with Meriken gentleman, as it seems to me, is his great lack in the verily tragic quality. A man without it is like oatmeal without salt.

(By the way—what a shame I can't make out my latter without "by the way"!—I am taking oatmeal every morning. How sad it doesn't show any sign of fattening me!)

O Oscar, can't you be jealous once in a while?

It will be fatal if you cannot, I am sure.

Why should I say my thanks for your box of candies? Oh, no, my dear old man! Honestly the candies began their savage work of spoiling my teeth before the box was half cleared away.

Can you adore any toothless girl?

Suppose I have false teeth—ones like Mother Schuyler's (don't tell her I know it, for goodness' sake)?

How shocking it will be if I drop them in my laughter!

It will be a shame if I put them back upside down in my haste.

Surely it will be the disgrace of all Japan if I ever go out in the street without any tooth, having lost my false ones. Girls always lose their particularly important things, you know.

Oscar, why don't you send me a bouquet of violets?

The flowers may die before reaching me, you say?

Naturally.

Still, it would be better so. I could cling to the dead flower, and cry, dreaming over its glorious yesterday.

Am I. sentimental, Oscar, as the newspapers said of my picture?

I thank you for the notice you sent.

Did you really place my picture in the California Spring exhibit?

Well, well!

Have I a suggestive face, as the critic says? What sort of face is it, I wonder?

Does it mean that my face lacks something?

I thank God, however, for giving me a nose, at least.

"A face delightful to artists"?

Do artists like such an incomplete face like mine? Really?

You must put me in a chamber darkened by heavy draperies, and lighted by just four candles, if I ever marry you. I have no doubt that any deficiencies will be pleasingly supplied by the mystery.

Don't feed me more than three grains of rice each day!

It would be romantic, if you should burn some incense—mind you, Oscar, not any Chinese one,—every evening when the nun-like stars hurry to the prayer-hall of the sky on tiptoe. Isn't it the very time for your devotions unto me?

Did you ever recite a prayer in your life, Oscar?

Yesterday I was scanning over a Sunday edition. I came upon the page for children with the big heading: "Boys and Girls."

"Boys and girls," Oscar!

Why in the world should "Boy and Girls" ever turn to "Ladies and Gentlemen"?

There's no other reason, if not that all the boys begin to degenerate after twenty.

I fancy no one can keep pace with an artist in degeneration. Has he, I wonder, any other work beside sketching and writing loveletters?

I am so glad you don't wear long hair.

I have read in the paper that the bacillus of love hides in the long hair of gentlemen and works a mischief upon the woman-heart.

Does Paderewski really wear long hair? Are women so crazy with him? I wonder how girls do look upon Mr. Heine?

If your love should ever be in your hair, and not in your heart!

Oscar, I know that youare true.

How can you be another way?

Do you know I do cry and cry sometimes over your sweet letter?

I am ready to cry my eyes out even now, if I didn't have to attend the front door.

Madam has no sympathy with a maid in tears, I'm pretty sure.

Your

Morning Glory.

(Parlor-maid to the Stuart-Dodges.)

P. S.—What jolly comrades I have nowadays!

Nothing could be more innocent than our heart-to-heart talks, Oscar.

We discussed only a while ago whether it was better to sweep before dusting, or to dust before sweeping.

Isn't it fascinating?

As I left the kitchen, my young lady—I will regard it as an insult, Oscar, if you ever ask whether she is lovely,—returned, crying, "Mother, we had such a discussion, Oh dear!"

God knows what it was.

I am positive, however, that "Is Marriage a Failure?" wasn't the subject, because she is too young for such a stupidity.

We girls discuss too much, don't we, Oscar?

How I wish I could send my biggest love to dear Olive!

Does she find out that we are loving each other?

2nd P. S.—I enclose a few strands of my hair and also a few silk threads.

Now tell me, Oscar, which is thread and which is hair?

Can you show yourself bright enough to distinguish between them?

Precious few gentlemen have such discrimination, I am told. Is it true?

A certain Oriental sage said that women's hair was strong enough to pull an elephant from the jungle.

Could my hair be strong enough to pull out my dear Mr, Ellis, I wonder?

M. G.

Letter XVII

6th.

O Matsuba, wasn't that awful?

What a mistake!

Shame on M. G!

The letter must have gone as far as Chicago, when I found it out.

If such a letter had fallen into my papas hands! You can imagine what would happen.

Wasn't it God's kindness that it fell into yours, instead?

I can see distinctly your satirical smile in the air, though.

For pity's sake, don't ask me how serious I was in writing!

Is it not said that girls my be forgiven if they write what they don't think?

Is it not a common thing for Meriken girl to shake hands coldly with the young man she once loved, since married to another?

Let me confess that I can't help loving Oscar!

I received your letter yesterday, Pine Leaf.

How I wish to write again on Japanese paper like that you use. What a soft-eyed face it uplifts to me!

Isn't it disgusting to feel the unsympathetic touch of stiff 'Merican paper with your hand?

What do you say when you see the blue lines parading across the sheet?

You will not blame me for using such inartistic paper when I tell you that I hardly know where to start wirh my writing, as the American paper appears like a football ground—perhaps the one I saw in Chicago—where I never know where to traverse. I will be safely guided on the lined sheet. My writing will be bound to follow the line like a runaway horse in the city which can only trample through the street.

Isn't this envelope dreadfully big?

You will be ready, I know, to fancy it may be from the government of U. S. A., appointing you as a professoress of flower-decoration.

Isn't it the whole business of the Japanese government to uglify things?

The whole 'Merican people is at home in such a respect.

Your Morning Glory is tremendously affected by it. What a pity!

I have been looking sadly at the ink bottle upon my table.

Isn't it too bad, Matsuba, it costs only five cents?

Why not one dollar, I say?

You shall be sick for a week if you ever lick your pen after using it as one does with a Japanese writing brush. Such a taste!

What fragrance in the Japanese ink!

(I don't say either Chinese ink or Indian ink, but Japanese ink, pine Leaf.)

What delight I took in grinding up the ink in a stone saucer! Didn't I gather the dews from flowers for the purpose, believing they would help to better my writing?

O Matsuba, is your engagement with Mr. Counsellor of the Foreign office really broken?

It was my opinion that such a gentleman had hopelessly turned to a show-piece upon the tokonoma. Doesn't his whole occupation consist of putting his feet upon the table, smoking a cigar, and swearing at the press criticism of the foreign policy? He keeps a geisha's card in his pocket generally. What a shame!

I would rather marry a peanut-seller, pine Leaf.

Do I want an American husband, you ask?

I am afraid, I confess, that Mr. American may be acting.

I have a silly fancy, sometimes, or how it would be to appear in a divorce court—is it not inevitable in Amerikey?—wholly forgetting my English. Everything slips from my mind in

My friend, can you believe this is a servant's room—this light room on the third floor?

What a distinction it would be in Japan to live on the third floor! The higher the thing—Emperor's chair included—the worthier it grows, doesn't it?

I couldn't believe it probable at first, when I heard that the family's rooms are on the floor below us.

Convenience is the keynote in American household arrangements, I guess.

Look at the white sheets of my bed

Even the servants' sheets are changed once a week.

We have no mouse at all.

How I miss one funny poison pedler of Japanese streets calling aloud! "No mouse? No rascal in your house?"

It is about the time, if this were Tokio, for the street singer—wearing her customary straw slippers—to come along singing an old love song of a forgotten city.

How sweet to have your mind carried away into romance!

The saddest part, however, is that every story of ancient Japan is a tragedy.

I think that tragedy is awfully out of fashion, like a world-worn genius.

What use to be sad, anyhow?

Such a vast greyness of New York streets!

The uninteresting monotony would make you insane if an organ-grinder didn't volunteer to break it once in a while.

Dear Dago!

(All the girls call the organ-grinder Dago. Do yon know why?)

You face meets only a procession of carriages, if you push it out from my window.

Ten thousand carriages, look!

Aren't you glad they are all grand ones, almost approaching to that of our Augustness?

Now, Matsuba, I have only twenty minutes before my evening work.

Let me fix a Japanese woman's picture, "Ofuku San celebrating a cetsubun," which was given me by Mr. stuart Dodge!

Setsubun—that is the last night of the year, isn't it?

Lucky picture!

Do you remember how we used to quarrel in gathering the beans on the setsubun, when my grandpapa threw them into all the corners of the house where an evil spirit might be hidden, exclaiming: "Oniwa soto!"

I posted the picture upon my door, and wrote:

"Devils be out!"

P. S.—You were so kind to invite me to join in the poem contest to be held at the Imperial palace.

How can I, dear pine Leaf?

The subject, you say, is "Tortoise and Bamboo"?

Pity M. G.! She has forgotten what the bamboo looks like.

Success, Matsuba!

Are you still attending a cooking-school?

Miss Cissy took the rôle of a housewife today, winding an apron about her.

Mary declared her a "nuisance."

The young lady advised her to put a bit more salt in her biscuit.

Mary was displeased with Miss Cissy's lecture upon the "Relation Between a Cook's Character and her Seasoning."

What temperament does Mary's occasional forgetfulness in seasoning indicate?

Miss Cissy eulogised the cook's profession as the highest art.

Can Mary be an artist, I wonder?

Letter XVIII

My dear Pine Leaf:

All the family have gone to their church.

You may be sure that Madam never leaves the church before the service is over.

Marianna said that Madam would be displeased if we worked hard. "Day of taking-it-easy" she declared Sunday. Madam once discharged a girl, so Marianna said, simply on account of her hanging the washing on Sunday at Nantucket Island.

(Nantucket is Madam's Summer place.)

The educated Ann promised me a heavenly season on the island. She asked me half a hundred times how long I shall stay with the family. Did I tell the truth? Oh, no, my Matsuba!

Isn't this country wonderful?

Can you believe that even a washerwoman wears a silken skirt here?

It is supposed in Japan that she cannot afford a cotton tabi even in Winter, isn't it?

Alice went to church looking more important than a Japanese mayor's honorable wife. She wasn't pleased, however, when Henry said, "Shall I get a few more buttons for you?" on seeing such a tasteless group of buttons on her shirt-front.

Nell comfortably stationed herself in the telephone room, and began a flirtattion with a fellow.

Is there anything longer than servant girl's telephone talk?

Poor Lucinda finally gave up her hope, after patient waiting of her turn with the telephone. She went upstairs silently, and a moment later began to play on Miss Cissy's piano.

The piece was "Waiting," she said.

She must be waiting for luck, that dreaming Lucinda.

"If God were only so particular like Madam on my pay-day!" She used to complain. Poor girl!

"No girl could made a better wife than Lucinda," was Marianna's recommendation. Isn't she bright with her needle? Isn't it the first duty of a housewife to worry about her neighbor's affairs? Isn't she ready to take all the family's trouble on herself? She came into the pantry this morning to ask how many chops Madam had eaten.

I withdrew to my room for the delight of one charming book.

What book do you guess?

"Alice's Adventures in Wonderland."

(I found it a week ago in the library.)

Did you ever hear of such a book? How could you, living under ever so much stupid gevernment who only allows the importation of Wilson's Geometry?

Dear little Alice, always managing herself the best way she can!

Didn't she give herself very good advice?

Poor always uncomfortable girl, ever wondering what will happen next!

Wasn't she inquisitive?

What politeness!

What delicious suspense I felt on my first reading! Did I read before such a clever book in my life? No, Pine Leaf!

I wrote a letter abundantly thanking the author. I even proposed myself to his publishers for a Japanese agent, thinking that the book should be placed in every school of whole Nippon.

Wasn't I tempted to be its translator?

What a shame!

The publishers returned my letter, supplying a little note about "Lewis Carroll."

Oya, the author had been dead many a year!

"Did I come here to show my ignorance?" I almost cried.

What mortification!

Can you imagine what a terrible letter I wrote to Uncle, denouncing his negligence in telling me about the book as the cause of my being thrown in such a pit?

Poor Uncle!

He is always to blame.

The carriage came back from church just as I finished the "Mock Turtle's Story."

Deeply sighing Mr. Mock Turtle, sitting sad and lonely!

"Thank you, sir! Some other time for your quadrille dance, however. I got to go now, as Madam has returned," I said with a bow.

I felt myself another Alice, truly.

DID YOU EVER SEE SISTERS of Charity?

O Matsuba, what heavenliness! Don't they look like a lingering dream of the nobler and sweeter past? Aren't they a picture of self-denial?

Look at their cap!

Indeed it does hint of the wings of a bird (to be sure a "Paradise birdie" white like a lotos). Are they not fleeing birds from the purer realm? Aren't they angels moving to the music of impulse?

Mary said that her Bishop ranks the work of charity as the highest.

I thought it would be an addition to the heavenly pages of my adventure, if I could chance to live with the Sisters.

If I could softly move around the sick gentlemen in white and black!

Why cannot my warm hands soothe the place where their pain lies?

The "patta, petta" of my footsteps—supposing that I walk the corridor on my bare feet of golden nudity,—cannot but echo in their suffering brains.

Isn't it glorious to be a woman?

How I wish I could work influence over a gentleman!

Pine Leaf, isn't it funny the Sisters are always two together in the street? They never step out alone. Like mandarin ducks in the lily pond?

What a scandal it would be, I fancied, if one of them were a man in woman's garb!

It would be more romantic if they were pretty girls.

Such homely ones!

I'm certain they will never blush under the gaze of the handsome men of the city.

Mary was almost crazy from joy, when they visited our kitchen.

(One of them was called Sister Euphrasia. What a mediaeval smell the name smells!)

Mary proclaimed that it was the only chance to have our souls saved, when they sent around the contribution-book.

I wouldn't mind giving my money, I said to myself, if I were permitted to try on their robe for once.

It was my temptation ever since I first saw one in Frisco.

Did I contribute money? Yes, Matsuba.

I couldn't make myself courageous enough to ask about their dress. Wasn't it too bad?

How they giggled!

I was so glad that they left just as I was inclining to be suspicious of their holiness. Are they really different from us?

How could I help adoring them, however, as they serenely threaded their way through the crowd on Fifth Avenue!

Undoubtedly they are a mystery of another existence.

I ran upstairs to my room. I saw them off till they disappeared.

Letter XIX

8th.

Miss Cissy and her company dropped into the art gallery for awhile.

She ordered Henry to bring five glasses of ice water.

A moment later the butler brought back all the glasses, being told that they did not need them after all.

"There's no question about their getting worse," he growled.

What difference is there, I should like to know, between the "young ladies" and us servant girls, if they can't change their minds freely.

Poor servant girls!

We have to be particular as keys. Are we not prompt like a mouse-trap?

The advantage of being an American lady is that people do not censure whatever she talks about.

Why should she make herself a martyr of boredom like a Jap musume?

O Matsuba, look up through the night! Isn't there a sign of dawn?

Why shouldn't we Oriental girls have our revolution?

What are Miss Cissy and her friend talking about, do you suppose?

They began, very likely, with telling how much weight they lost in the past week.

Do they know each other's ages?

How can I be positive that I will tell truth when I am twenty-five.

"What a stupid lecture it was," one girl will exclaim with authority.

Where in the world is a clever lecture? Lecture isn't lecture, if not stupid, I dare say.

She must have left the lecture hall before the lecture was half-finished. Didn't she regret that she had to take the 9.30 train when she left?

Poor poet!

Mr. Heine ever complained that nearly all the ladies of his "remarkably intelligent audience" always took that "devilishly interesting" 9.30 train.

Presently another girl will tell how she can't help pitying the Poet Laureate of England for his printing of such an awful poem.

Isn't it too bad for him that people must denounce his qualifications simply for the sake of being looked upon as "literary?"

Why shouldn't he do hara-kiri for his eternal flight from insult?

He isn't Japanese, Pine Leaf.

I bet you he was mistaken in his selection of a wife.

It is not enough to say that a poet's wife is always clever enough to pick up a splendid poem from her husband's waste-basket. Doesn't she always correct his poems? Doesn't she verily often write for him?

Where's Mrs. Laureate, anyhow?

It would do him a world of good,—I don't mind a bit advising him— if he could write something upon the Meriken girls.

How sad it is, my Matsuba, that he looks so much like my dear papa!

The face, you know, as if eating a sour apple.

Don't I feel insulted when one speaks ill of him?

Now you must suppose the young ladies are leaving the art gallery.

Dear Pine Leaf, it is the moment for us to steal in, when "soft stillness and the night become the touches of sweet harmony."

Do you want to take off your shoes, Matsuba?

I agree with you in calling it the holy place.

"How heroically pathetic!" will be your first exclamation, on seeing a picture of a beautiful girl holding the iron rod of a prison cell.

Isn't she Charlotte Corday?

What a girlish docility still flaps around her mouth! What a wild splendor fires her eyes!

Do you remember how we cried reading over her history in our school? Didn't I wonder how I could show such heroism at twenty-five?

Pine Leaf, I am always scared by a large cow when I turn round. She does gaze at me so.

Did you ever see one?

Are you still keeping on nice terms with our old painter (you know whom I mean) who is so delighted to chat about his meeting with the great Corot in his old Paris days?

"What an aureole in his white hair! He carried such a simple linen parasol," he always said, didn't he?

Most suddenly my fancy's eyes will see an old man before me, when I glance over Corot's "A Spring woodland."

His eyes dance like a sparrow's, Matsuba. He will pause every three minutes, and look round the tree, occasionally throwing his kisses, you know. Has he picked another secret from Nature, I wonder? I shouldn't be a bit surprised if he began to talk with the bird.

Let us turn to Millet's picture.

Don't you see the miserable scene of his Barbizon home in your imagination.

How many pictures are here altogether, do you suppose? One hundred and fifty. Isn't it wonderful?

You will not forget to look at Lefebvre's "Morning Glory" for my honor's sake.

Does the girl look like me? What glorious hair! I must put something in my bosom when I go out next time, because woman should have an ample breast to look attractive. Mine is so poor. How sad! What shall I put? Newspapers do?

I will turn out the light, leaving the whole gallery in the hands of the ghosts slipped out of the pictures.

Is it the voice of Turner that I hear?

No, my girl, it must be Sir Joshus.

Wait a minute, Pine Leaf. Pretty soon we shall hear Gainsborough. He was so handsome when he was young, don't you know?

REALLY, TODAY IS THE EIGHTH of April, Matsuba.

I have been almost forgetting about the honorable birthday of the Lord Buddha.

(Am I Buddhist? No, dear, I'm nearer to Christian.)

What a delight I had, nevertheless, in helping the priests build a tiny flower-house in honour of the baby Buddha!

Which kimono did you wear in visiting your temple?

How were our sweet genge flowers this year? Did you use the dandelion plenteously for the house?

Is it not a prophecy of your marriage this Autumn, if you come across a white genge while you are picking?

How many cups of "sweet tea" did you pour over the image?

Isn't it a dear little baby?

I wish I could get just one cup of the "sweet tea." Madam grieved over the riot of cockroaches. Doesn't the incantation written with sweet tea forbid the presence of any insect?

I wrote it, however, with ink. I pasted the paper behind the door. I will see how it turns out.

Nell awfully complained of her being caught by an undesirable visitor tonight, and consulted me about how to make him leave.

Wasn't I ready to help her?

I gathered six broomsticks, and set them on their handles in the kitchen.

Isn't it a charm in such a case?

What a shame it didn't work very well!

I bade Nell to sneeze three times for my next charm's operation.

Then I jumped into the room, and tapped on her shoulders one dozen times. "Go right upstairs, and never come down again, Nell! If you do? You will catch cold within a minute," I said.

The poor fellow was left alone.

Letter XX

My beloved Matsuba:

Aren't you disgusted with my letters so unpardonably wanton?

It's all due to my mistake in not learning sobriety while writing essays in school.

Will you send me a book of Japanese letter writing?

How do you do, Matsuba Sama?

(You must suppose, now, I bowed to you—well, quite nicely.)

How I miss the pine tree, living in an American house! My dear Miss Pine Leaf, of course! What a delicious greenness in the Japanese pine!

Wasn't I glad to find one in Mr. Stuart-Dodge's garden?

Directly I hurried toward it, hoping I might hear the familiar song of pine leaves.

Oya, Meriken tree is dumb, Matsuba.

Not one flake of breeze in New York City, I reckon.

I have been reading the following lines written upon a vase in the drawing room:

> "April, pride of murmuring
> Winds of Spring,
> That beneath the winnowed air
> Trap with subtle nets and sweet
> Flora's feet,
> Flora's feet, the fleet and fair. . ."

O Pine Leaf, I long for my Japanese April! Dearest season for the cherry blossoms! What a glory in the sunlight! Such an odour in the wind!

Didn't we cry when the day was finally sent beyond the sky?

Didn't we exclaim that we were turning into a flower that was nothing but Life!

Do you remember how once we rose at dawn and planted a sign amid the cherry-trees of Ueno Park, proclaiming that we were the first callers? Such fun!

Really I am homesick. How can I help it?

Is it lovely today in Japan as in New York?

It is this very day that you will have "the honorable-looking-at-each-other" with Mr. Intended-to-be-your-husband under the cherry-trees upon the bank of Sumida River.

(You said so in your letter, didn't you?)

Don't be shy in your inspection of him, my dear girl!

Mark his moustache above everything.

It is but inconstancy in him if it is reddish.

You should examine what he keeps in his tobacco-purse, if any chance offers.

I don't like a gentleman that carries a cane, do you?

Matsuba, you must never forget to see what a divination-slip (tsujiura) says, before giving your decision of yea or nay.

I used to be perfectly wild to buy the tsujiura, whenever a vendor passed by at night calling:

"Awajishima kayo chidorino koino tsujiura!"

(Love-divination by a plover crossing over to Awaji Isle!)

Look at the vendor's lantern!

Doesn't it strike you as a waving divine will if you see it in the darkness?

O Pine Leaf, didn't you make me promise to inform you what an American blacksmith looks like, as soon as ever I came across one?

Honestly I have been watching for him many a month.

I came upon him most suddenly yesterday.

It was right by the Stuart-Dodges' back entrance.

Wasn't it our dream ever since we read Longfellow's poem? Didn't our professor emphasize that the real Americanism was enfolded in that one piece? "Dear blacksmith," we cried. How crazy we were to see the Meriken face that "looks the whole world in the face, for he owes not any man"!

What a disappointment that my neighbour's shop didn't stand under a chestnut-tree!

It is a city smithy, Matsuba.

Was his hair "crisp, and black, and long"?

Alas, no! I was glad, however, to observe that his brow was moistened with sweat.

Has he children?

Matsuba, I called on him today.

"Your sweet wife must be dead, I fancy. Does your daughter sing in the choir on Sunday? Doesn't her voice sound like your wife's singing in Paradise?" I said.

He flung his fearful look.

"I'm unmarried, I tell you," he exclaimed.

What a shame!

This afternoon I went down to the laundry (in the cellar) to do some washing.

Did you ever wash yourself? I suppose not.

Why don't you, Pine Leaf?

Are you afraid your hands may grow coarse skinned?

(I sadly confess that my adventure wholly ruined my fingers.)

Can you believe that the Stuart-Dodges use Ivory soap for their washing?

It means, Matsuba, that they spend three Jap policemen's honorable salary for just soap every month.

Alice kept singing:

> *"As fair art thou, my bonnie lass,*
> *So deep in luve am I;*
> *And I will luve thee still my dear,*
> *Till a the seas gang dry."*

Is it not Burns?

I avoided talking of poetry, because my stock of Burns was exceedingly poor.

But I had to laugh on finding that all the poems Alice ever knew was only that one.

"The most ekstravagant gyurl you are, Morning Glory!" she exclaimed, seeing my silk stockings in the tub.

"Now I know why all the gyurls call you the most high-tone parlor-maid."

Really, do they?

Wasn't I tickled to death?

It is easy enough for me to be a servant, Pine Leaf, but the difficult problem is surely how I can manage with my wages.

How much did I spend already, do you suppose?

(I will not forget that I loaned one dollar to Miss Cissy last night. Think! What use to be a millionaire's daughter, if she can't have such a small money herself?)

Look at those heavy irons!

Do you think you could handle them cleverly?

How can I know how hot they should be!

Lo, I burned terribly one of my undergarments.

Wasn't I quick to wrap it in a newspaper?

Presently I slipped away from the laundry carrying it upstairs. I was afraid that Alice might find out my complete ignorance of ironing.

You see I am pretending to be a through-bred servant-girl.

Letter XXI

Yahoya hoya, sora yenya!

This is my day out, my honorable girl.

Nell San will join me.

She was done with theatres through and through, as she said. It was her belief that play was no play at all, without a villain. She mournfully lamented that modern theatre has utterly turned into a dress show. She would step right into a dressmaker's shop, if she wanted a new style, she declared. How indignantly she asked "Does a different dress make a different character? No, sir!"

I gave up my thought of persuading her into a theatre.

Must I carry a pistol with me?

O Matsuba, can you form any idea what a barbarous place "Noo Yoik" is? It's anarchy. Look at the newspapers! Isn't it dreadful that they are filled with accounts of missing girls?

It would be fatal if I ever went out into the streets in my kimono. What a mighty temptation I should be for the kidnappers! There's no question about it they would take me for another "Madam Butterfly."

(Uncle said that the play—"Butterfly" is now acted on the stage, you know—was the saddest creation in the world, being a jam of burlesque and pathos. He could hardly stand such craziness, he said.)

I must appear as a non-Japanese as cleverly as I can.

I am a bit vain to say that I am quite at home with such a make-up.

I never can understand, however, why Japanese in Amerikey acknowledge it as praise to be told that they are not taken for Japs.

Are they thinking they are a poorer race, I wonder?

Pine Leaf, isn't it funny that the missing girls always wear four diamond rings and a gold breastpin set with rich sapphires?

I am told that any actress, to grow to a leading lady, must be lost three times a least.

Divorce has become commonplace in advertising.

Everything in this country is going in the style of "feast-day show of Asakusa's Love Goddess," you see.

I'm sure that I should be put down as "Mikado's daughter run away from the Tokio Palace," in my advertisement.

What jucket did I wear, you ask?

"My! Morning Glory, you are just as pretty as Miss Cissy. What elegant clothes you got! Look!" dear Marianna exclaimed, carried away by astonishment when I stood ready in the kitchen

"Aren't they great?" I said, displaying the silver embroidery of morning glories—what a deliciously uncertain gesticulation of the cup and leaves!—down the front from the inside collar. They were done by a Japanese artist in Frisco.

(By the bye, the jacket is of Persian lamb.)

I know that you would have a little appreciation of gold buttons and gold tags upon the collars and sleeves.

"Let us go quick!"

Nell was so excited, rushing down stairs.

I was told, afterward, that a certain Mr. Professional humorist—whose name no girl cares to remember—had just called on Stuart-Dodge. What does it matter? He was everything evil, so Nell said. She lost a thing or two, whenever he came. Postage-stamps were the beginning and her love-letters the last. "God knows what I am going to lose next," she said.

You are sure that the honorable Mr. Humourist looks like an undertaker.

Isn't it a Japanese saying that a humorist and a priest at a funeral are twins in face?

I forgot my handkerchief.

Was it because the humorist was a visitor, really?

We walked down Broadway.

Can you imagine how enthusiastic the gentlemen were in looking at me?

I couldn't help feeling quite nervous.

"Is my hat on straight?" I asked Nell.

My hat!

It had a Louis XV bow in front.

But it is the fashion for girls to wear a picture hat. The hat itself is supposed to give an advantage of sixty per cent for even a girl on trial for her life.

The streets were lighted.

Nell looked so positive with her "charming face" under the yellow light.

O Matsuba, what fun it is to cross a street and to be rescued by an enormous policeman from being run over by a car!

Where am I now, do you fancy?

Twenty Third Street.

Didn't I make myself a laughing stock by mistaking a waxwork figure for the real thing when I stumbled in front of a show window? How seriously I did beg pardon for my misdemeanor of stepping on his foot!

You shall see Nell, presently, hugely admiring the pups of a dog-seller. Her first question was how old they were, of course. Didn't she even suggest the names for them? By and by, she will leave somebody's address—goodness knows it wasn't hers—for one dog sent C. O. D.

Isn't she awful?

Oh, what a crowd!

We are marching toward the Bowery through Fourteenth Street.

Such an excitement!

It would be more interesting if a pickpocket woud work on me, I thought.

I observed that Nell was protecting with her hand a gold crescent embellished with a line of pearls.

Why is she so careful?

Are, ma, such girl!

She was using Miss Cissy's jewel without her consent.

Did you ever?

A moment later you will see us sitting in a fortune-teller's den.

Did you ever see any gipsy woman in your life, Pine Leaf?

How glad we were to be told many a thousand nice things!

"Wonderful!" Nell exclaimed, ready to be sentimental over her love affairs.

Didn't I lavish my pennies for a peep-show?

Certainly I gave my money to all the beggars I came across.

Wasn't I delighted to kiss their babies, if Nell hadn't held my arm, saying, "Shame on you!"

Dear Matsuba, it is about the time when we become hungry.

We stepped up into a wagon.

Alas! It was a lunch house.

I wouldn't mind spending ten dollars if I could make the wagon move along the street.

What a pleasing dizziness, what a muddle-headed rapture I felt!

My coffee spilled all over the table, while my eyes were following the monstrous demonstrations of the Bowery through the green window of the wagon.

I had hard work bringing the lunch-wagon keeper to agree to give one hand-broken coffee cup for half a dollar.

Immediately our whirling heads were turned toward our Fifth Avenue.

I chose a dusky street on account of carrying the honorable souvenir.

"Yes. Nell, I must drop into the Park, and rest for awhile," I insisted. What an abrupt stepping into Poetry, whose quietude is a superior change! What a silent song of stars!

Poor Henry!

He was paitiently waiting for our return.

I was disappointed, however, to find that our preparation of a great barrel for the occasion when we must crawl into the kitchen window was useless. Didn't Mary leave one door unlocked!

I had a chicken bone ready for Sir Charles when he should come noisily upon us, taking us for thieves.

(The kitchen and stable are close together, you know.)

"So kind of you, Henry," I said.

I threw my kisses to him, bidding him "good-night."

We stripped off our shoes, and calmly stole into our chambers.

"Where's my coffee cup?" I said as I laid my wearied body in my bed.

O Morning Glory, you left it in Central Park,—upon the bench.

Letter XXII

"Onino inaiuchi,
Sendaku shimasho!
Gosh, gosh, gosh!"

Let us wash, while devils be away! Gosh, gosh, gosh!)

What an outburst of hilarity!

All the family had gone to pass the day with their relative in New Jersey.

Nell seized me tight, violently insisting upon giving me a few lessons on how to do a cakewalk. What a tremendously frolicsome melodys she began to whistle! What ridicuously fantastical steps she took! We turned round the kitchen table—I clumsily tripped, to be frank, not knowing how to step. The newest "two-step" song is "My Hello Girl," she said.

What's a "Hello Girl," do you guess?

Telephone operator, my dear.

She is said to be particularly clever, being skillful to put any mount of pathos in that one "Hello."

Mary the cook began this holiday by treating the butcher's boy to breakfast.

She was on the point of bringing out a dining-room chair, when Henry severely opposed such an action.

You will see her, presently, going upstairs for her one-hour bath. Didn't she leave the words, "Tell any gentleman who may call that *Miss* Mary will be down after a little while?" Certainly she did.

God knows who will call!

She will make her appearance, by and by, in a white muslin dress. How could she forget to put her watch upon her breast! I wish she wouldn't wear such a brass belt with bits of green glass on it.

O Matsuba, she did even put powder on her face.

Think of face powder in the forenoon! Isn't it as crazy as a parasol under the snow?

She will settle herself on a rocking chair before the stove, and shortly start her humming.

Isn't it her "Every Day is Sunday"?

The educated Ann wouldn't condescend to come down. She was so much occupied with her solitaire, doubtless.

Solitaire!

What a thrillingly melancholy affair it is, you can imagine!

Lucinda went out to a post-office to send five dollars to her mother. Isn't she sweet?

I saw Marianna going out, afterward. Really she looked like a dowager in a farce, wearing such a fur coat. She paid thirty dollars for it, so Nell said. I fancied that she intended to make it her heirloom. How careless she was, not to take a lorgnette and fan with her! She couldn't be complete without them, I'm certain.

"Whose birthday is today?" Mary said suddenly at the luncheon table.

"Mine!" I exclaimed not seeing any possibility of its being any other girl's

Was I born on this day?

Let me confess that I never know my own birthday!

Didn't my papa tell me the date?

I gave up trying to remember it, however, since I found out that my brain was not serviceable at all.

Didn't I say that any day in heavenly April would be perfectly adaptable for it?

Did I feel guilty, you say, when all the girls grew so enthusiastic to celebrate It in my honor?

Oh, no, iya, Pine Leaf!

I was singularly delighted to fancy that I was born on such a lovely day as this.

I should say that it would be romantic if I could forget the year also, eternally keeping me in nineteen.

I made my own will,—for fun, you know. I forbade my family to put the date of my death on my tombstone. I did beg them to burn perfume, and present flowers, whenever the cherry blossoms opened and the moon was large. The words on my stone would be "Here lies M. G., who did not know when she was born."

I loosed my hair, when I found myself in my room. I ventured to create a new mode in my coiffure. Why could I not take up a certain Japanese style with an alteration? The result would be admirable, I said, if the Oriental stiffness were replaced by a free-minded downiness.

The papers never lose a minute in chronicling any new thing.

All the girls are looking for a change.

Wouldn't it be great if I could popularize "The Morning Glory"— supposing I call my style so,—in Moriken society?

My name will be in every mouth.

Just think!

Did I try shimada? Marumage?

I hardly think any curly hair is fit for those.

"Three rings"?

Perhaps.

Tenjinmage! That's the very one. Is it not that my two looped tresses should be held down by a hairpin forced through a third at the crown?

Immediately you will see my hair done like the following sketch.

Isn't it a clever variation?

It will make a sure hit, I dare say.

My comrades begged to be taught its process.

Did I tell them?

No, sir!

A birth-day cake was brought out, after the supper. Mary set it before me.

All the girls wished me many happy returns.

Did I make a little speech, you ask?

No, my dear Matsuba, I was afraid that no girl who only weighs one hundred pounds could be weighty enough to impress by her oratory.

Marianna bade me blow out the candle-light. I divided the cake evenly.

Oya, Oyaoya!

I found a ring in my slice of cake.

"Morning Glory, you shall marry within two years. Didn't your two blows put out the light?" Nell exclaimed.

Lucinda girl was awfully sulky, seeing a bean in her cake. "I do not want a farmer for my husband. What a shame!" she complained.

"May I keep this ring?" I said.

"No, Morning Glory, that's mine, Marianna was prompt to answer.

"My dear, what will you say, now? Will you still say no, when I want you to exchange it for my ring? Gilded, you say? Did it cost you only half a dollar? What does it matter? I like to keep it as a remembrance," I said, when I brought down one of my gold rings, and put it in Marianna's ever so large palm.

"You are a great girl," all the girls were breathless in exclaiming.

Later on, I introduced a Amida-kuji (Buddha lottery), when they were starting to put up money for the ice-cream.

Alas, my ticket was blank. Didn't it mean that I was to go on the errand?

I called a hansom-cab when I appeared in the street, bidding: "Take me to the best candy store in town!"

Pine Leaf, you must suppose now I returned to the Stuart-Dodges.'

"Say, Jimmy or Joe—whatever it be,—come right down, and join with us for the ice-cream! Henry! Oh, Henry, watch the horse for a while for him!" I exclaimed.

Dear Henry!

"Look here, girls! I have a present for each one."

I piled up eight one-dollar boxes of candy upon the table.

"Oh, my goodness! Morning Glory!"

Look at those startling eight pairs of round eyes!

O Matsuba, honestly I never felt so happy before in my life as tonight,

I couldn't slumber long in my bed. I kept buzzing a nonsensical song:

"Yosakoi yosakoi,
Sora don don don, sesse!"

Letter XXIII

Dear Matsuba,

What an excitement it was when Zara made her abrupt appearance showing a kitten!

Mah, mah!

Did you ever see such a proud gait?

"Zara! O Zara!" we all cried.

Miss Cissy was a trifle dissatisfied with the kitten's homely face with no eye.

Our sensation was doubled when Zara renewed her exhibition with a second one.

Are they all?

A carriage stopped as I was stepping down stairs carrying a piece of silk to make a cushion for Zara's babies.

Didn't I "crush my soul" hearing Uncle's voice in the front hall?

My Lord!

Matsuba, O Matsuba!

What should I do? Hide me in a closet?

How terribly my body shook!

Presently Madam called loudly, "Morning Glory! Morning Glory!"

Can yon imagine how I felt fearing what might become of me?

There was my eternally dear Mr. Minister smiling abundantly.

"Now, Morning Glory, you got enough of adventure, haven't you? You must come with us, my dear girl. Our steamer leaves within a week, you know," He spoke in old-fashioned fatherliness.

I was awfully glad my honourable uncle—ever so careless gentleman about his dress—didn't come in his Japan-made suit, which was disgustingly unfit.

"Uncle, my month isn't up yet," I said, sadly.

A moment later, I looked upon Mr. Minister with a smile, and said: "Tell me, how do I look with my cap? Is it becoming?"

Precious old man!

It seemed to me that he and Mr. Stuart-Dodge were verily well known to each other. Mr. S.—D. didn't tell me that. Such a mean gentleman!

"Morning Glory, you would better go upstairs. I told Nell to help you get ready. Now take off you cap, and turn again into a nice Japanese lady," Madam said, affectionately caressing my hair.

She was examining my hair, I fancied, being still doubtfull of its genuine quality.

Pine Leaf, she was so lovely.

What an agitation I made among the girls, you can imagine!

All the girls peeped out from the drapery of the breakfast room.

I asked Madam not to forget to pay my wages. I told her that I would not accept anything but a bank-check.

Marianna caught me at the foot of the back-stairway, exclaiming: "Morning Glory, I thought for a long time that you were not of the same class with us. You were such a mystery, my great girl."

I inscribed my name behind the door of my room as a memory.

What a simple Nell!

She did not know how to help me, she was so tremendously moved by my gorgeous kimonos.

When I was all ready, I went down again into the drawing room, where the three gentlemen were absorbed in their talk. You are sure that Mr. Minister began with "the good friendship between Amerikey and Japan." Of course he looked delighted in telling about the increase of our commerce.

That is all every minister got to say, you know,

Did he forget to praise Miss Cissy, I wonder?

"Are you ready, Morning Glory?" Uncle said.

"Mr. Coachman turn the carriage to the kitchen door, if you please," I entreated.

"Girls, I'm sorry that I got to leave!" I exclaimed.

Didn't I kiss them all?

Dear old Marianna?

She was almost crying when she wished me happiness.

How she prayed that I would write her once in a while!

Miss Cissy rushed down with a bouquet of red roses.

To be sure we kissed each other.

"By-bye, Morning Glory!"

"May I expect you tomorrow at the hotel, Cissy?"

Just a minute, gentlemen, pray!

I must see Zara's kittens again.

Letter XXIV

13th.

My adventure is all over, Matsuba.

I must have been sleeping, while my hair-dresser was busying herself behind me.

Am I not awfully tired?

Letter XXV

L'Envoi.

I invited Cissy for luncheon.

She is a sweet one, Pine Leaf. Isn't she interesting like a rich menu of this Waldorf?

How brightly her eyes shine!

She honored me promising to name the kittens "Morning" and "Glory."

"Did your mother get another girl in my place?" I asked.

"She got one homely enough to be a married woman," she said.

Isn't it funny that we think only a homely girl gets married?

16th

Let me walk down Broadway again!

Dear old church beyond the city Hall! I must drop in there again, and breathe the purple silence as from another world.

Shall I throw my kisses to the statue of Horace Greely?

Wouldn't it be more romantic if Broadway were wrapped by the fogs at evening like Frisco streets?

It is like a gentleman without any trick, plain and grand.

When can I see you again, my beloved Broadway?

17th.

O Matsuba, don't Japanese call Amerikey "the Country of Stars"?

The following seventeen syllables are my far well poem:

> *"Hoshiwo mitsu,*
> *Narewo omowan,*
> *Haruno yoru."*

(Looking at the stars, I will remind me of thee, every night of Spring.)

I put the following lines in the "Personals" of one paper:

"Sayonara, Meriken girls!

M. G."

今より千秋と相待申候、

明治卅八年二月

草々

逍遙

野口詞兄

彼れが天眞流露の日本
才女を紹介して彼國の
風流士をあくがれさせ
たる裏をゆきて、此れは
彼方の内幕を筆に活動
の寫眞畵なるべければ、
いづれかといへば故郷
人を驚かす微妙じき士
産なるべくや、神ならぬ
身の此の常推量中るや
否やを知らず、令嬢より
の小包の解かれん日を

境遇が境遇だけに一切
が覓かに高潔なるバメ
ラ式ならんかとも豫想
いたし候、觀察の奇警周
細、これもまた彼の小フ
ン二ー以外か乃至は以
上かいづれにしてもは、
あて皆まで言ふに及
ず、その邊は老生承知と
御尊父御保證の事と存
候、何はしかれ、今度のは
前の「日記」とは別樣の御
用意あることとなるべし、

存候、とりわけバージス
某への思ひはせぶり、平民
式のミッス,カグャはさつ
てもとんだ罪を作るも
のかなと我れ知らず感
歎浅からず候ひし、それ
も何時か既往となつて、
今度おめでたき「宮仕へ」
察するところ今より以
後は、彼のカルテンを妻
げて看るマウント何と
やらの雪などはふんだ
んのわざくれなるべく、

で此の年ばへに斯うま
ではと舌を巻き候程の
洒脱聰慧、無盡藏の才華
は、何の事は無し、五彩に
迸る火花の如く、又獨得
の愛敬は如何な情無し
の鬼神をもついへなへ
なに萎し候はんと存ぜ
られ、如何さま、メリケン、
ヨーロッパのハイカラ
連の貴なる賤しきが愛
で惑つて、氣をもみくち
やにせしこと尤至極と

坪内博士
の書簡

拝啓令愛朝顔嬢には弥
〻メリケンの大家へ御
奉公なされ候由承り及
び候、さて〱東西文壇
の慶事、抃賀千万回の儀
に御座候、今更ながら彼
の君の「日記」を讀み候て
は、例の春は曙のおもと
二十世紀に生れて海老
茶袴穿いたりともいか

A Note About the Author

Yone Noguchi (1875–1947) was a Japanese poet, novelist, and critic who wrote in both English and Japanese. Born in Tsushima, he studied the works of Thomas Carlyle and Herbert Spencer at Keio University in Tokyo, where he also practiced Zen and wrote haiku. In 1893, he moved to San Francisco and began working at a newspaper established by Japanese exiles. Under the tutelage of Joaquin Miller, an Oakland-based writer and outdoorsman, Noguchi came into his own as a poet. He published two collections in 1897 before moving to New York via Chicago. In 1901, he published *The American Diary of a Japanese Girl*, his debut novel. Noguchi soon tired of America, however, and sailed to England where he published a third book of poems and made connections with such writers as William Butler Yeats and Thomas Hardy. Reinvigorated and determined to continue his career, he returned to New York in 1903, but left for Japan the following year following the end of his marriage to journalist and educator Léonie Gilmour, with whom he had a son. As the Russo-Japanese War brought his nation onto the world stage, Noguchi became known as a literary critic for the *Japan Times* and focused on advising such Western playwrights as Yeats to study the classical Noh drama. He spent the second decade of the century as a prominent international lecturer, mainly in Europe and Britain. In 1920, Noguchi published *Japanese Hokkus*, a collection of short poems, before turning his attention to Japanese-language verse. As Japan moved closer toward war with the West, Noguchi turned from leftist politics to the nationalism supported by his country's leaders, straining his relationship with Bengali poet Rabindranath Tagore and distancing himself from his former colleagues around the world. In 1945, his home in Tokyo was destroyed in the devastating American firebombing of the city; he died only two years later, having reconnected with his son Isamu.

A Note from the Publisher

Spanning many genres, from non-fiction essays to literature classics to children's books and lyric poetry, Mint Edition books showcase the master works of our time in a modern new package. The text is freshly typeset, is clean and easy to read, and features a new note about the author in each volume. Many books also include exclusive new introductory material. Every book boasts a striking new cover, which makes it as appropriate for collecting as it is for gift giving. Mint Edition books are only printed when a reader orders them, so natural resources are not wasted. We're proud that our books are never manufactured in excess and exist only in the exact quantity they need to be read and enjoyed. To learn more and view our library, go to minteditionbooks.com

bookfinity & MINT EDITIONS

Enjoy more of your favorite classics with Bookfinity,
a new search and discovery experience for readers.
With Bookfinity, you can discover more vintage
literature for your collection, find your Reader Type,
track books you've read or want to read,
and add reviews to your favorite books.
Visit www.bookfinity.com, and click on
Take the Quiz to get started.

Don't forget to follow us
@bookfinityofficial and @mint_editions